Turn

It UP!

Jen Calonita

Scholastic Inc.

ISBN 978-1-338-27712-8

10 9 8 7 6 5 4 3 2 1   18 19 20 21 22

Printed in the U.S.A.   40
First printing 2018

Book design by Maeve Norton

For Pattie Ann Leibman and my
friends at the Dance Place

CHAPTER ONE

Lidia

WERP!

The noise was so loud, Lidia Sato almost fell out of her bed.

She sat up and stared sleepily at the Sailor Moon alarm clock on her nightstand.

It was only 6:52 a.m.! And that noise sounded like it was coming from inside the house!

EEEE—WERP!

There it was again! What was that noise? Didn't her family realize she was still sleeping? Her alarm wasn't due to go off for another eight minutes!

Lidia coveted sleep the way her mother loved chocolate, her brother collected Pokémon cards, and her grandmother had a daily date with *The Price Is Right*.

SCREECH!

Lidia covered her ears with her pillow. The sound reminded her of nails on a chalkboard, but she wasn't at school. She was home in bed.

She pinched herself to make sure. Yep, still in bed. Where had she heard this noise before?

EEEE!

Aha! Suddenly, the sleep fog lifted and the answer was clear. That was the sound of a mic being plugged into an amp that someone had forgot was turned on. But Lidia had to be wrong. No one in her house would be stupid enough to plug in an amp this early.

"Good morning, Naples, Florida!" Lidia heard her ten-year-old brother, Douglas, yell into a microphone.

Lidia groaned. Sleep was now a lost cause. Anyway, it was almost time to get ready for her job as a first mate/unofficial cruise director/ member of the fun squad on Salty Sam's pirate tourist cruise. She stretched her sore limbs, pulled back her plaid lavender comforter, and jumped out of bed. Pushing her long black hair out of her eyes, she slipped her feet into her fuzzy rainbow-colored slippers. Wait till she got her hands on Douglas!

"We are coming to you live from the Sato household where Evie Fukui will now be singing her number-one Japanese pop hit, 'Bubble Gum Love.' Take it away, Evie!"

Evie? Her grandmother was in on this pre-alarm travesty too?

"No, *you* take it away, Douglas Sato!" Lidia heard her grandmother say. "I'm making lunches. I can't solo right now."

"Come on, Grandma! It's just one song!" Douglas begged. There was something about his caramel-coated voice that let him get away with murder. "Please? I need to practice my guitar solo before lessons this afternoon, and 'Bubble Gum Love' is my favorite song to play."

Dougie was such a kiss-up.

"Aww, all right. Let me just put this turkey sandwich in your lunch box and I'll warm up my voice." Lidia rolled her eyes—Grandma Evie never passed up the chance to hold a mic. Her grandmother began a series of warm-ups at full volume.

It was official. Her family was insane.

Sure, her family kept a karaoke machine in the dining room the way other families had a china cabinet, and it wasn't unheard of for someone to break out the microphone while washing dishes, but pre-alarm a.m. jam sessions needed to be banned. Lidia would mention this at dinner that night, but she knew she wouldn't win the argument. Music was her family's life and there was no escaping it.

Everyone at Bradley Academy, where she went to school (and where her mom was headmistress), loved studying at Lidia's because there was always a chance someone would burst into song, like they were secretly being taped for a Japanese American version of *The Partridge Family* (Grandma Evie's second favorite show after *The Price Is Right*). It also didn't hurt that the Satos lived on campus in one of the faculty houses. Instead of holing up in the tomb-like library, students could walk to Lidia's in five minutes flat and be serenaded.

RIP! The growl of Douglas's guitar solo kicked in as Lidia walked slowly to her closet to get dressed. She winced when he strummed the wrong chord.

"Wait for me! I just have to brush my teeth!" Lidia heard her mom shout. "I'll be down in time for the chorus."

"I'll grab my acoustic!" her dad added. She could hear him running down the hall. He banged on Lidia's door. "Lidie, up and at 'em! Family jam session over Cheerios starts now!"

Lidia banged her head against her closet door over and over again. How could her family love to sing this much?

Lidia *liked* to sing. If she didn't, she and her best friend, Sydney, wouldn't have lobbied to become co-captains of Bradley Academy's all-female a cappella group, the Nightingales, this coming sophomore year. They'd dreamed of a cappella gold and glory since they'd started at the upper campus in seventh grade. Lidia's mom—who had been in Bradley's original Nightingales back in the day—still talked about how the group made her high school experience and how much fun a cappella competitions were. But by the time Lidia and Sydney joined freshman year, the Nightingales' reign was over. Still the girls weren't worried. They had a plan to turn the group around and bring home the team's first trophy in years at the a cappella kickoff competition, Turn It Up, in November.

"If we win at Turn It Up, then we'll move on to the next a cappella competition and then the next, and before you know it, we will be taking home the golden fruit at the Orange Grove Championship next May," Sydney had declared. She was so sure of this, she had made Lidia a papier-mâché Orange Grove trophy. It sat on Lidia's dresser along with Sydney's other gifts, like "best friend forever" cards, Sailor Moon tees (since she knew Lidia was obsessed with the character), and even her old iPod, loading it up with new songs they could use for the Nightingales.

If they got enough girls to join the group.

Lidia shook her head clear of the negative thoughts Sydney hated. ("Don't jinx us!" she'd say. She was way more positive than Lidia was about these things.) But it was hard not to be skeptical that the Nightingales would make it another year. Last year, they'd barely had enough members to remain a group. Most of the team had graduated in June, leaving them with a handful of returning sophomores and juniors they'd have to convince to sign up again.

They were in tenth grade now and Syd's dream had never wavered. But if Lidia was being honest with herself, *her* faith in the Nightingales had. She was secretly convinced the group would fold, so she'd started taking dance classes at school and at Integral Dance Arts. She'd wanted to have something that would look good on college applications in case her a cappella career was over, but then the strangest thing happened: She fell in love with dance. This past summer, she'd even bumped up her classes to four a week. After her shift at Salty Sam's, she'd run to hip-hop on Mondays, ballet on Tuesdays, a contemporary dance class on Wednesdays, and an acrobatics class on Thursdays—she couldn't decide which class she liked more. It didn't matter. She'd have to cut back to one the following week when school and Nightingales practice started up again. As co-captains, she and Syd would be working on songs and arrangements after school four days a week.

It killed her to think about giving up her dance classes, but every time she tried to tell Syd how she felt, she choked. Her best friend lived and breathed the Nightingales. How could she tell her that she wanted to have time for things other than singing? Syd had them sharing earbuds to listen to music, picking songs that wouldn't make the judges scream "No more Gaga!" and watching a cappella YouTube videos from winning groups as near as Port St. Lucie and as far away as Portugal.

Lidia smiled to herself. Only Syd could be that obsessive and still be her charming self. Her best friend was going to make a great actress/singer someday.

It was Lidia who didn't know what she wanted to be yet, and sometimes that worried her.

"Your smile makes my gum go pop, pop, pop!" Grandma Evie sang at the top of her lungs as Douglas chimed in on his guitar. As promised, Mom came in on the chorus as did Dad and his guitar. "Lidia, get down here!" her grandmother sang.

No one was allowed to sit out the music in the Sato house. Maybe her friends were right. The Satos were missing out on their chance to be the musical Kardashians.

Lidia started dancing around her closet to the beat. She had to admit it—her grandmother's song was catchy. She turned on the light in her closet and contemplated clothing options for the Gulf Coast in mid-August. Next week, she'd be back to wearing her pale-blue-and-yellow-plaid uniform, but today she was happy to slip on a gray tank top and slouchy silk shorts. They showed off the dancer's legs she'd earned by doing a hundred scissor kicks in a row and two hundred pliés nightly for the last two months. After years of hating her tall, lanky frame, she was now embracing what her dance school owner called "the perfect dancer's body."

By the time she got downstairs, the jam session had ended and everyone was sitting around the kitchen table.

"Lidia!" Douglas complained when he saw her. He was still in pajamas. "What took you so long? You even missed the encore!"

"We could always do a second encore," Grandma Evie suggested as Mom, Dad, and Douglas took turns pouring cereal. "In my day, Popmore Fun came back out onstage as often as our fans begged us to." Her grandmother's perfectly drawn-in black eyebrows went up.

Her grandmother didn't look sixty-five. With short, cropped black hair, a face full of makeup even at breakfast, and cute, stylish sweaters that even Lidia wanted to borrow, her grandmother looked more like some of the moms at school pickup. "Music has kept me young," her grandmother always said whenever anyone complimented her appearance. She'd been in a pop group growing up in Japan, but when she came to America she had settled on giving music lessons instead of playing herself so she could raise Lidia's mom.

"Maybe later," Lidia promised. Singing with her grandmother was a kick.

"Lidia has to rest her voice." Her mom looked at her appraisingly with her dark eyes. "Nightingales practices are less than two weeks away!" She let out a cheer and banged her spoon against her orange juice, making it slosh around in the glass. Her mom's own Nightingales trophies still sat proudly in her home office.

"Mom, practices only resume *if* we get enough kids at auditions and can put together a team," Lidia reminded her.

"Yeah, and the Nightingales are the most unpopular group at school," Douglas said as he shoveled cereal into his mouth. Milk

7

dripped down his chin. "It's even more unpopular than the badminton club."

"That's not true!" Lidia said in horror.

But deep down she knew it was true. Painfully true.

Still, the entire family glared at Dougie for the traitor he was. "It *is* true! The Nightingales probably won't even have a team when I get to upper school." He smiled, revealing the gap in his two front teeth. "It will just be me and my awesome Kingfishers."

"You sound as sour as this grapefruit, Douglas," their dad said. "The Nightingales are returning to glory this year. We can feel it." Everyone but Douglas banged their spoons against their juice glasses. Lidia couldn't help but join in. She banged her spoon the hardest, then felt her phone buzz. She looked at the screen and saw the photo of Syd looking very diva-ish in mid-song with a mic practically touching her lips. There was a text.

> Wake up, sleepyhead! Meet me at Don't Be Crabby's for iced chai lattes before our shift. We're celebrating! Dad said I could host a prospective Nightingales event at the shop! YAY!

"Breakfast?" Grandma Evie asked.

"No thanks. I'm going to meet Sydney at Don't Be Crabby's before the boat cruise."

Everyone started talking at once.

Her mom fired questions rapidly: "Did you and Syd discuss

audition songs yet? Did you take my suggestion? You can't go wrong with 'Catch My Breath' by Kelly Clarkson."

"So overdone!" Grandma Evie disagreed. "I think my Little Big Town's song choices give girls all sorts of range."

"Grandma Evie, you listen to Little Big Town?" Douglas asked.

Grandma Evie smiled proudly. "I listen to everything! Those Chainsmokers are a talented bunch too."

"All of your suggestions are contenders, but we haven't narrowed down our choices yet," Lidia said diplomatically. Syd was always saying Lidia was the peacekeeper. Lidia had convinced Shannon Todd to sing a duet with Annette Bryant at last year's spring concert even after Annette called Shannon's voice "pitchy" in the school vlog. "Maybe we'll decide at breakfast."

"Good idea," Grandma Evie said. "Better take our suggestions before the Kingfishers snatch up all the best songs." The family muttered in agreement. "Speaking of Kingfishers, have you seen that Griffin boy lately?"

"Grandma!" Lidia's cheeks started to burn. "We're just friends." *Actually, we're not even friends, but I do know all there is to know about him through Sydney*, she thought.

"I was just curious," Grandma Evie said innocently. "Should the rest of us do one more song before work? I charged my favorite gold mic." Dougie and her dad jumped right up to jam.

That was Lidia's cue to exit. She kissed her mom on the cheek, rushed to the kitchen's back door, and kicked off her slippers. Sliding into her flip-flops, she grabbed her cinch bag with her pirate uniform and eye patch. (She never changed into it till she was on the boat. Too many comments from people trying to be funny. And Lidia's family was enough comedy for one day.)

School wasn't in session, but thanks to the summer camp, the Bradley Academy shuttle buses still ran. Lidia caught the one that went to downtown Naples. Slipping into an unoccupied seat, she stared out the window as the bus wound its way through the Bradley Academy grounds, passing empty manicured lawns, the lake, and rows of palm trees that would soon give shade to the campers who thought it would be fun to eat lunch outside. It wasn't.

Lidia stuck her earbuds in her ears and pulled up the new Nightingales playlist Syd had sent her the night before. This one was titled NIGHTINGALES VICTORY TUNES!, which was way more confident than the prior week's list, which was called SAVE THE NIGHTINGALES! Lidia laughed to herself. Syd had been her best friend since they met in fifth grade chorus. Even though she could drive her crazier than anyone else on the planet—including her own *Partridge Family*—Lidia wouldn't change Syd for the world.

Well, maybe there was one thing.

Syd was impossible to say no to. She'd been pushing Lidia to talk to Griffin Mancini since Lidia first started crushing on him in eighth grade. When Griffin sang "Billie Jean" at the school talent show, he picked Lidia out of the audience to sing to. It was just an act, she knew, but it was enough to create a love spark that had grown into a bonfire over the years. She liked him even if he was a prankster for the Kingfishers and liked to brag about his voice (kind of like Sydney).

Lidia likened it to her obsession with Justin Bieber. She knew loving him was wrong, but she couldn't quit the habit.

And yet, she still hadn't worked up the nerve to have a conversation with Griffin that lasted longer than their time on the lunch line. "Are you going to take the last Jell-O?" was not a line that was going to get her noticed.

She knew Syd's pushiness was just her way of trying to help. Griffin and Syd had gotten parts in the Naples Community Theater production of *In the Heights* over the summer, and Syd kept inviting Lidia to rehearsals so she could get to know Griffin better. But whenever Lidia tried to talk to Griffin, she clammed up.

But it was a new year and Lidia knew it was time to make some changes. She would talk to Griffin. No, not just talk: She'd flirt! Syd said he was funny. Well, she'd be funny too. Funny and flirty and he wouldn't be able to resist her!

When the bus reached the pier, Lidia hopped off and walked the short distance to Don't Be Crabby's. Syd wasn't supposed to meet her for another fifteen minutes, but Lidia would snag a table. When Syd got there, she'd be proud of Lidia for having all her notes about auditions spread out.

The air-conditioning hit Lidia in the face as soon as she opened the door. The shop was crowded, but she spotted an empty table in the back, which looked out over the pirate ship she and Syd worked on. Lidia quickly walked toward it and got trapped behind a mother with a double stroller. *Don't take the last table*, she thought to herself, silently cheering when the stroller moved. She dashed for the empty seats. But she stopped short just a few feet later when she spotted Sydney already seated at a table nearby.

Griffin was with her.

Lidia's heart did a one-handed cartwheel at the sight of him in a royal-blue tee and board shorts.

But before she could even open her mouth to say hi to either of them, she watched in seemingly slow motion as Griffin leaned across the table and kissed Sydney on the lips for all of the coffee shop to see.

Lidia's heart felt like it had stopped in her chest. She stood there for a moment, completely confused and upset, then quickly snapped out of it and, in a daze, turned around, crashing into that stroller and sending someone's glass flying off their table and shattering to the floor. *They're going to see me*, she thought.

"Sorry," she mumbled quickly and rushed out of the coffee house. She didn't stop running till she reached the bus stop. She couldn't show up at Salty Sam's now.

All Lidia could think about was that kiss. A kiss that should have been meant for her.

CHAPTER TWO

Sydney

LID—WHERE ARE U???????

Sydney texted Lidia for what felt like the millionth time in the past two days and got no response.

On Tuesday, Lidia didn't show up at Don't Be Crabby's before their shift on Salty Sam's pirate cruise, which wasn't like her. Lidia was never late and always handed in assignments—including a list of prospective Nightingales Sydney had suggested compiling—way early. And she never flaked out on work, unlike Sydney (who had already gotten a written warning). That is why Sydney was sure something had happened to her. A quick call to Lidia's house had calmed her fears. Lidia's grandmother said she was sick. But a person could be sick and still answer the phone or respond to a text, couldn't they? Lidia hadn't done either.

It was as if . . .

No. Not possible.

Griffin.

The name popped into Sydney's mind before she could stop it and her stomach fluttered. *Traitor!* she yelled at herself even as her mind flashed to some of her favorite summer memories, which all seemed to include Griffin. They'd spent so much time together rehearsing for *In the Heights* that it was bound to happen: They clicked. She'd only started chatting with him to get more intel for Lidia, but she quickly realized she and Griffin had a lot in common. They both had a jug at home marked HAMILTON where they squirreled away money to go to New York and get tickets to see the Broadway show. They were both obsessed with *Grocery Wars*, this bizarre coupon-cutting reality show. They agreed that they fell in love with musicals when they saw *Singing in the Rain* as kids. Even musically, they were in sync. When a song they liked came on the radio during rehearsals, they both burst out in song, matching harmonies without even trying.

Griffin.

Don't even think his name, she reprimanded herself. *It was a stupid mistake. It's never going to happen again.*

From now on, she'd refer to him as He Who Shall Not Be Named. Griffin Mancini was as dangerous as Voldemort.

Ugh! She'd said Griffin's name again!

And again! Why did she keep saying Grif—

ENOUGH! What had happened at Don't Be Crabby's had completely messed with her head. One minute she was grabbing a table for her and Lidia, all proud of herself for being the early one for a change. The next, He Who Shall Not Be Named had stopped by to talk about the latest episode of *Grocery Wars*. They started laughing over something that had happened with detergent and then he had blurted out how much he liked her. Sydney was stunned. He was supposed to like Lidia! Just when she was about to tell him that, he'd leaned across the table and kissed her.

Sydney had been so freaked out, she'd left the coffee shop without even getting her coffee. She'd texted Lidia that she was running late for their pirate shift and gone straight to the boat, her heart pounding and her lips still tingling from the memory of what had just happened. Or, as she kept telling herself, *hadn't* happened. Sydney wanted to wipe the memory from existence just like that time in fifth grade when she tried to sing falsetto during her solo in the holiday concert. He Who Shall Not Be Named was not hers to think about. Lidia had been in love with him forever.

You need to tell her what happened, a little voice pressed.

No! Sydney told herself. *Lidia would be crushed. And besides, it didn't mean anything.*

Sydney glanced at her phone again. No response from Lidia.

Above her, the town hall clock chimed four. She couldn't wait any longer. She had to get to Pinocchio's. It was time to convince some girls to become Nightingales!

Ever since she and Lidia began dreaming of being Nightingales co-captains, they'd been keeping tabs on potential new sopranos, altos, and beatboxers—girls they'd spied singing in the halls or to the radio. Sure, most of these girls had never been in chorus before, let alone expressed interest in joining an a cappella group, but if they got just the right mix of singers to join, the Nightingales could be on their

15

way to a cappella glory again. Sydney could actually see herself holding a trophy at Turn It Up. Lidia was the one who came up with the idea of inviting girls to hear about the Nightingales before school started, and that's when Sydney suggested her dad's ice cream shop, Pinocchio's. She'd even gotten him to agree to give out free (small) sundaes. Together they'd put up a post online saying *FREE ICE CREAM! BRADLEY GIRLS ONLY!** And then in smaller print had explained: **And while you're eating your sundae, hear us explain why the Nightingales is the group you WANT to be in this year!*

Twenty-five girls had commented they were coming. That was more than twice as many girls as they needed to have a group! Two girls they didn't love—Micayla and Whitney—had RSVP'd as well. The gruesome twosome had tried, and failed, to beat her and Lidia out as co-captains—so Sydney expected them to do their worst to try to derail the meeting. But still—twenty-five girls were coming!

Once they were all there, Sydney would give "The Big Speech" about how incredible it was to be in a singing, dancing, all-girl group. (Sisterhood! Solidarity! Togetherness! Fun!) Then she and Lidia would dive into their rendition of "For Good" from *Wicked*. The girls would be so impressed that they'd want to know more about the group, and that's when Lidia was going to tell them how being a Nightingale would give them confidence onstage, which would help them in college interviews, and in the Run the World jobs they'd someday have. Sydney smiled to herself. She may have been the actress, but it was Lidia who nailed public speaking. Between the two of them, this meeting couldn't go wrong.

She just needed to make sure Lidia was coming. Sydney pulled out her phone again to text Lidia and saw the little circles under the message spin. Lidia was writing back! Then the circles disappeared. What was up with Lidia?

Sydney pushed her pale-blond hair off the back of her neck and fanned herself with her Nightingales notebook. It was *so hot* out, she was starting to melt, and there was still no sign of Lidia on the busy street.

She would never understand why her dad loved living in southwest Florida. Sure, her parents had met at Florida State University, but why didn't they leave the state afterward? Who chose *Florida*— with its alligators, retirees, way too much Coppertone, and too little culture—to raise a family? When her parents divorced and her mom moved to Philadelphia, Sydney thought her dad might pick up and move somewhere new too, but he'd stayed put to open Pinocchio's.

The first chance Sydney got after graduation, she was out of here. She was headed to New York, Los Angeles, or any culturally cool town that had more than one stage production a season. She would not work in Orlando at a theme park singing for peanuts. She had bigger dreams. And those dreams included living outside the Sunshine State.

Syd clutched her purple polka-dot notebook to her chest. The book had all their notes, plans, and dreams on those pages, and Sydney never let the notebook out of her sight. During *In the Heights* practices, He Who Shall Not Be Named had even teased her about it.

She felt buzzing in her bag. *Lidia?* She pulled her phone out, read the text, and frowned. Then smiled. Then frowned again as her heart beat faster. Speak of the devil.

GRIFFIN: You can't ignore my texts forever.

GRIFFIN: School starts next week, which means you'll soon be forced to talk/fawn all over me in person.

GRIFFIN: But it would be less awkward if we talked about what happened first. Call me, okay? I'm sorry if I freaked you out.

GRIFFIN: But not sorry because I've wanted to do that all summer.

So he wasn't sorry he'd kissed her. This was BAD. Really bad. Lidia was going to find out. Sydney had to shut this discussion down ASAP.

SYDNEY: Nothing to talk about. Forget it even happened. Please.

GRIFFIN: I don't want to forget. Can we please talk about this?

GRIFFIN: Maybe over an episode of Grocery Wars?

Why couldn't this happen with a different boy? Not that she'd found any boys at Bradley Academy that got her the way Griffin did, but Griffin wasn't hers to like. She wanted to reply so badly, but she knew she shouldn't text him. She reluctantly put her phone away.

She needed to stay focused on the Nightingales. With any luck, Lidia was already at Pinocchio's wooing a group of girls over a salted-caramel sundae with marshmallow sauce (Lidia's personal favorite). Lidia was great at explaining things in a way that put people at ease, whereas Sydney tended to be a bit hyper about everything.

Sydney walked down the block, thinking about the afternoon game plan. If they could convince Julie Ivarone and Natalie Chen to try out, Angela Burt and Sophie Higgens would want to come too. Then the freshman class would get wind that it was cool to be a Nightingale and there would be a flood of auditions. They'd have to turn people away!

She threw herself through the front door of Pinocchio's and spotted her dad behind the counter taking orders. "Hey, kid," he said, like always. (Sometimes she wondered if he even remembered her name.) He smiled as he bent over the ice cream in the freezer, giving her a glimpse of his thinning salt-and-pepper hair. "Lidia and some other girls are already in the back waiting for you. Good luck!"

Lidia was there! *Good*.

"Thanks, Dad! I promise to work some shifts this weekend to make up for all the ice cream!" Sydney slipped past the barn door that separated the ice cream shop from the private room normally used for kids' parties and smiled when she saw the large (large!) group of girls in the back room. Julie and Natalie were there with

Angela and Sophie. YES! So were Viola Chasez and Gabby Cyprus, fellow sophomores who were always nice. There were also some girls in the junior class like Yvonne Poj and Kelly Moira, who sang Beatles songs on a field trip last spring and sounded amazing. And . . . oh no. Pearl Robbins was there. She'd tried out last year and didn't make the group. She remembered Pearl being super pitchy. And who was she talking to? Did that girl with the wavy black hair have a puppet on her right hand? Sydney started to panic. What if they were forced to take Pearl and Puppet Girl because they didn't have enough girls for a team?

She was being ridiculous. Auditions were going to be great! The turnout for the get-together was even better than Sydney could have hoped for. It was time to put Operation: Save the Nightingales into action.

She spotted Lidia sitting at the soda shop counter in the back of the room, her long legs dangling from the spinning counter stool, and headed over. Gabby was saying something to her that the other girls nearby were riveted by.

"And that's why this group is cursed," Sydney heard Gabby say.

The word "cursed" stopped Sydney in her tracks.

"No. Way," said Sophie, her jaw dropping slightly. "You're telling me Vanessa Pyun was blown off the stage and broke three ribs when she landed in the orchestra pit?"

"Yes," Gabby said solemnly. "It was as if a giant gust of wind came out of nowhere and carried her off. I saw it myself."

"She was spinning, Gabs," Viola said with an eye roll, running a hand through her short, curly hair. The two were good friends. "I don't remember the wind."

"There was wind," Gabby insisted, her arms waving wildly and her bracelets sliding up her arms. "The Nightingales are cursed."

Throughout all this, Lidia had remained silent. If she wasn't going to step in with all this cursed talk, Sydney had to. She laughed extra-hard. "Gabby, you're hilarious! No one was blown off a stage! The Nightingales are not cursed." Her voice sounded pitchy rather than confident. She never sounded pitchy! "That's just a rumor the Kingfishers started last year to get back at us for *supposedly* toilet papering every member's house the night before spring break. Right, Lidia?"

Lidia spun around on the bar stool, not saying a word. *Okay.*

Gabby shook her head slightly, her short brown bob barely moving. Sydney suspected she shellacked it to keep it from frizzing in the Florida humidity. "If the Nightingales aren't cursed, then how do you explain the season when Hurricane Charlie flooded the Bradley Academy Performing Arts Center?" She looked at the other girls. "The group had to practice in the cafeteria all season, and their pitch was so off, they didn't place in any competitions."

"I heard they didn't place because they barely had enough people to keep a group going," said Yvonne, walking up behind them. "No offense, Sydney, but the Nightingales don't have the best reputation."

"Well, that's changing with me and Lidia in charge!" Sydney nudged Lidia, who spun away from her. What was going on? "Besides, everyone knows the cafeteria has terrible acoustics."

"How do you explain 2014?" Gabby pressed. "That year my sister was in the group and the Nightingales somehow made it to the state finals."

"They were great that year," Sydney said, but no one seemed to be listening. Instead, more girls gathered around Gabby.

"The group was hungry so they stopped to eat on the road," Gabby told them. "And that is how the Serrano Tex-Mex Grill Food Poisoning Incident happened."

"I heard their club advisor picked the place for lunch and stepped down afterward," Natalie volunteered.

"Mr. Matthews's wife got a job in Utah and they had to move," Sydney said in exasperation. "And it wasn't food poisoning. It was just a team-wide stomach virus."

"There's a difference?" Yvonne asked.

"Yes!" Sydney said wearily. "We're lucky Mr. Matthews left. Mr. Wickey's a way better advisor anyway—he racked up tons of awards in his own a cappella collegiate career."

Gabby cut her off. "But nothing was as bad as what happened last year. Ariel Simon, the lead vocalist, left the group right before competition season to try out for *The Voice*." There was a murmur of excitement. "She didn't make the cut and was so embarrassed, she left school. Someone said she moved to Long Island, New York, and is now on Word of Mouth." She shook her head again. "I'm telling you, this group is cursed."

Grr . . . Sydney tried to stay calm. "If that's true, then why did you come to hear about auditions?"

Gabby grinned. "Are you kidding? Free ice cream! And besides, I love drama. This is better than trying out for the play. I want to be a Nightingale and see who falls victim to the curse next."

"There's no curse!" Sydney snapped. The girls all looked at her. Sydney smoothed her hair behind her ear. "I mean, accidents happen. Sometimes people have bad luck or a few bad a cappella seasons. It doesn't mean a whole group is cursed." She nudged Lidia. "Tell them, Lid."

Lidia jumped out of her chair. "I need ice cream. Anyone else want to make a sundae?"

What was she doing? They'd planned for speeches first, then ice cream. Lidia wasn't sticking to the plan, and now girls were following her across the room to the sundae bar.

Sydney felt a pat on the back. "I wouldn't worry about the curse this year, though," Gabby said brightly. "Look how many girls are here! There is going to be fierce competition for spots. Even Micayla and Whitney better bring their A game. Where are they anyway?"

"I don't know," Sydney said. Maybe they were so bitter about not being captains, they had changed their minds about the group.

"More ice cream for us," Gabby said. "Question: Would you allow dogs as background singers? Just at tryouts? I've taught mine to howl in harmony when I sing."

"Umm . . ." Sydney didn't know what to say. What was happening?

Gabby smiled. "I watch dogs as part of my family's doggie day care business."

23

"Cool," Sydney said. "If you'll excuse me, I wanted to get everyone's attention to—"

"Hi, Sydney!" said someone with a squeaky voice.

"Hi, Pearl." Sydney hoped her voice didn't betray her feelings.

Pearl bounded up to Sydney, practically engulfing her in a big hug. Her long, frizzy red hair moved in one motion, like she was wearing a helmet. "I'm so happy I got your text. I mean your post, but I'm just happy to be here!" She wrung her pale, freckled hands anxiously. "I wanted to say I've been working a lot on my pitch since last year's auditions and I think—THINK," she said, her voice cracking, "you'll love what you hear!"

"I'm sure I will," Sydney said, sidestepping her and quickly making her way over to Lidia, who was spiraling whipped cream on top of a five-scoop mint-chocolate-chip sundae.

"Is that for you?" Sydney had never seen Lidia eat a sundae that big, which was funny considering they could both have as much free ice cream as they wanted at her dad's shop.

"Yep." Lidia kept her eyes on the sundae, which she topped with chocolate pieces.

"Okay, well, are you ready for 'The Big Speech'?" Sydney whispered, adjusting her shoulder straps and the thin belt on her paisley-printed dress. She'd bought the dress because it was the same color as the Nightingales' group logo—lime green and blue.

"It's all yours," Lidia said, adding some gummies to her ice cream skyscraper. "I'm not really in the mood to talk today."

The plan was for Sydney to start, Lidia to jump in, then Sydney would do the big finish. They'd practiced it for weeks. "What's wrong? Are you feeling okay?"

Lidia finally looked Sydney's way and Sydney's stomach plummeted. Lidia always looked her best, even if it was for a sleepover, but today her normally sleek hair was frizzy and her eyes were swollen. It was as if . . . Sydney's heart began to pound faster.

"What do you think?" Lidia grabbed a fistful of jelly beans.

Lidia knows about Griffin. Sydney wasn't sure how, but she did.

Did she take the risk and come clean? She looked at Lidia. They'd been best friends for five years. They never kept secrets, which meant Sydney should tell her. *Just tell her!* her head screamed.

"I . . ." Sydney couldn't do this now in front of all those girls. "I . . . Did you bring the songbooks and the iPod?"

Lidia's face seemed to close up. "No."

"That's okay!" Sydney tried to act normal even though her heart was pounding out of her chest. "I'm sure I have the music on my phone." She pulled up the playlist and turned to the crowd. "Hi, everyone! Lidia and I are so happy you could hang out with us today."

Most of the girls turned away from the sundae bar, but a few were still adding toppings. The jelly beans were a huge hit. So was the whipped cream. Sydney strained to be heard over the noise of a container running out of air. She felt her phone buzz, but she ignored it.

"Bradley Academy has great extracurriculars for you to choose from, but the one we're hoping you'll consider this year is . . ."

The whipped cream container sputtered to a stop. Sydney heard a girl say, "Do you know if they have more?"

Her phone buzzed again, but she ignored it. ". . . the Nightingales." She smiled brightly, trying to remember to make eye contact with each and every girl. The Nightingales would be all about personal attention! "With me and Lidia as the new co-captains, we are sure this team is on its way back to the late-1990s glory days!"

"Is that how long it's been since this group won?" someone whispered as someone else dumped candy into a bowl.

Sydney was starting to feel sweaty. "But it's not just the songs and the arrangements that make this group fun. Or the competitions, which are cool as well. The Nightingales is a sisterhood. We look out for each other."

Lidia suddenly burst out laughing. "Sorry!" she told the others. "I was thinking of something funny."

Sydney was so thrown, she forgot her next line. She looked at Lidia helplessly, but Lidia had gone back to eating. Sydney could feel the sweat dripping down her back. She never got stage fright. What was happening to her? "It's going to be an amazing a cappella season and we hope you'll—"

Someone started coughing. Then another girl. Sophie spit out a jelly bean and held up the mushy red bean in her palm. "These taste like throw-up!" Sydney's phone buzzed again. *What was going on?* She pulled it out and read the string of texts.

GRIFFIN: You have been hit! I repeat: You have been hit! The Kingfishers got to your candy bar. DON'T EAT THE JELLY BEANS! They taste like barf!

GRIFFIN: Don't shoot the messenger. I didn't know!

GRIFFIN: Okay, I knew.

GRIFFIN: But then I felt guilty and told you! DON'T EAT
THE JELLY BEANS!

CHAPTER THREE

Lidia

Sydney let out a small yelp. Lidia looked up from her hot fudge sundae to find Sydney staring at her phone in horror.

"Thanks, Griffin!" she heard Syd mutter before diving onto the toppings table and sending candy flying. Girls shrieked and dove out of the way. "Don't eat the candy!" Syd said hysterically. Her green-and-blue paisley dress—the one Lidia had borrowed to wear to *In the Heights* to look good for her crush—was now covered in hot fudge and caramel sauce. "The Kingfishers swapped the jelly beans out for ones that taste like barf!"

Around the room, Lidia heard the lovely sounds of girls spitting out food into napkins or gagging.

"Why would the Kingfishers do that?" asked a ninth grader named Donna. The girl seemed sweet but was so quiet she was almost impossible to hear. On her right hand she had drawn in Sharpie a puppet she called Ms. Heel. Lidia noticed when Donna "pretended" to be Ms. Heel, her voice was much stronger. Lidia had no idea how this girl was going to survive auditions, but she believed everyone deserved a chance. Mr. Wickey had given one to Sydney and her, pulling them up to the Nightingales a year early in eighth grade, and Lidia always liked to return the favor. Who knew? Maybe the puppet could sing.

"They're our rivals!" Sydney scooped up the bowl of jelly beans and tossed them in the trash, then pulled apart the window blinds to look outside. "It's tradition for the two a cappella groups to prank each other, but this is going too far. Now they're starting before the season even begins!" She let the blinds drop and they banged against the glass. "Well, wait till they see how we retaliate." Sydney began texting. "Griffin and those guys don't know what they're in for. I don't care if he warned me!"

There was his name again. Sydney and Griffin were now kissing and texting right under Lidia's nose. Sydney didn't seem to care whether Lidia knew, but also didn't have the decency to tell her to her face. Her heart literally felt like it was being ripped in half.

"Griffin warned you about the jelly beans?" Lidia asked quietly.

Sydney's sun-kissed face grew pale. She dropped her phone onto the table as if it were on fire. "Yes, but . . ."

Over the past few days—which she'd spent in her dark room, lying under the covers until they started to smell because she hadn't showered—Lidia had gone over every possible scenario in her mind. But no matter how hard she tried to wish away what she had seen at Don't Be Crabby's, she knew there was no other explanation: The same Sydney who had said, "This will be the summer he finally realizes you're perfect for him! I'll make sure of it!" had fallen for Griffin herself.

Lidia was driving herself insane wondering how long it had been going on. Did they talk about what a fool she was for not seeing what was happening? Were they together on opening night when Sydney insisted Lidia talk to Griffin at the after-party? He and Sydney were both into some ridiculous show called *Grocery Wars*. Lidia had said she couldn't be bothered with reality TV and she and Griffin had run out of things to say. Was *Grocery Wars* the reason he was with Sydney and not her?

Now she was being ridiculous!

It didn't matter when they'd gotten together; the point was they were consciously talking behind her back. *Her* Griffin and *her* best friend. And neither had the decency to tell her.

"How often do you and Griffin text?" Lidia asked.

Lidia could see Sydney's heart was beating out of her chest. *Good.* She should be anxious. "Not often. Just about play stuff."

Lidia played coy. "Isn't the play over?" *Don't do this*, she told herself. *Not now.*

But she couldn't help getting worked up. She never should have come to Pinocchio's. She'd debated going, but she didn't want to let the Nightingales down. She'd promised she'd be there and she never broke her promises. Unlike Sydney.

Sydney's eyes darted around the room. It was clear the rest of the girls were listening. "Can we discuss this later?"

Lidia didn't care who heard. Maybe everyone there already knew the truth. "It's a simple question: The play is over, but you guys still talk?"

"Yes . . . I mean no . . . ," Sydney said hastily. "I don't know why he texted me and not you." Her cheeks were reddening.

Oh, Syd. Why can't you come clean? Lidia thought. *If you cared about our friendship at all, you'd come clean right now.*

"Can we get back to the meeting?" Sydney said. She looked at the others. Her hands were shaking. "I'm sorry about the jelly beans. You should all make new sundaes. I'll have my dad bring out more toppings that I'm sure aren't tampered with." Sydney opened the private room door and called out to him. "DAD! We need new toppings, please!" She closed the door again. "Great. All fixed. Everything is fine. Just fine!"

Things were not fine, and Lidia wasn't sure how much longer she could keep from screaming that out loud in front of everyone. But if she had an outburst, it would scare off potential Nightingales. They'd have no team. Lidia didn't want that to happen, but she was beginning to enjoy watching Sydney squirm.

"And the fun isn't over!" Sydney's laugh sounded fake. Maybe she wasn't as good an actress as Lidia thought she was.

Then again, she had pulled off dating Griffin behind Lidia's back.

"Lidia and I thought we'd give you a taste of what we've cooked up for this season." Sydney grabbed her iPhone and punched up the arrangement of "For Good" the two had spent weeks working on. Sydney started to sing.

Lidia was supposed to jump in on the third line. She didn't, because when she looked at Sydney, all she saw was that kiss. The

31

image hurt worse than anything had ever hurt her before. Her eyes began to well up with tears and her emotions started to bubble over. She had to get out of there. Now. She headed for the door.

"Lid?" Sydney stopped mid-verse. "Where are you going?"

"I can't be here right now." Lidia pulled the door open. Everyone was staring.

"Don't go," Sydney begged hoarsely. "We should talk."

"It's too late for that," Lidia said forcefully. Sydney could pretend to look all hurt and innocent, but Lidia knew the truth, and now she wanted her to hurt as bad as she did. "You made me look like a fool. I'm your best friend and you humiliated me," she said shakily. The girls in the room started whispering. "You kissed Griffin! The one boy I've liked forever!" The whispering grew louder.

Sydney's eyes widened. "Lidia, no! I . . ."

"No excuses! You kissed Griffin Mancini! I saw you!" The girls in the room were eating this up, but Lidia didn't care. "You knew how much I liked him, but that didn't stop you! You were my best friend! How could you do that to me?" The room was silent except for the sound of someone munching on what could only be Heath Bar crumbles.

"I *am* your best friend!" Sydney said, trying to reach for Lidia again. "Please let me explain."

"You are a liar," Lidia choked out. "No one in this room should trust a word coming out of your mouth." She was revved up now and couldn't stop. "Wonder why you're all here?" Lidia said to the others. "So she can talk you into being a Nightingale so the group doesn't fold. Well, maybe it should!" She looked at Sydney again. "You can't be trusted as captain. I'll never believe a word that comes out of your mouth again!"

Sydney looked horrified. "Lidia, let me tell you what really happened."

"I saw you with my own eyes," Lidia said, her heart racing faster. "You're on your own from here on out." She slammed the door behind her, and as she did she heard Gabby's voice very clearly.

"I told you this group was cursed," Gabby said.

Lidia didn't stop to hear any more. She just wanted to go home and crawl back in bed.

After she changed the sheets.

Thankfully, the bus home was pulling up as she reached the stop. Lidia jumped on, standing at the front of the bus for a moment to see if Sydney had followed. Not that she wanted her to, but she thought her supposed best friend might try.

But no Sydney appeared. She was probably too busy trying to save her reputation in front of potential Nightingales.

Lidia took a seat in the middle of the bus in an empty row and let the scene that had just unfolded wash over her. She'd told a roomful of girls from Bradley Academy that she had a crush on Griffin Mancini and that her best friend had kissed him.

What had she done?

She covered her face with her hands and practiced breathing in and out.

This was what she got for not talking to Sydney beforehand.

But why should she have said something? Sydney was the one who had torn their friendship apart! The internal fight with herself lasted the whole drive back to campus.

"Bradley Academy," the bus driver announced as he rolled to a stop at the gates to campus.

Lidia had been so lost in her own thoughts, she wasn't ready to get off. "Hold the door!" she yelled, grabbing her crossbody bag. Her headphones were strewn on the seat next to her along with her phone, which was blowing up with texts she was ignoring. She had her dance bag with her too, since she was originally going from Pinocchio's to class, but now she was done so early that she had the chance to go home first. She piled all the items up in her arms and tried to move fast, but the doors started to close anyway.

"Hold the door!" Lidia shouted, running up the aisle.

A boy stepped out into the aisle at the last second and the pair collided, Lidia's dance bag tumbling. She heard her jazz shoes slide under the seats as the bus doors shut.

"Come on!" Lidia groaned for more reasons than one.

"I'm sorry!" the boy said, reaching down at the same time as Lidia, their heads colliding.

"Ouch!" Lidia rubbed her head. Her anger from earlier nearly bubbled over. How much more could she take today? She looked up to glare at him. "Watch where you're go—oh."

The guy was pretty cute. He had black-rimmed glasses that were hanging crooked on his tan face, and dazed big brown eyes. His short, messy black hair looked like it hadn't been combed, which was kind of adorable, and he'd missed a button on the gray short-sleeve button-down shirt he was wearing with cargo shorts. The guys she knew from school wore tees with stupid sayings on them like CHICKS DIG STICKS (a lacrosse player favorite). This look was a definite improvement.

"Let me help you find your things," he said. "Hey, Carl? Can you hit the brake, please? We're getting off."

He knew the driver's name? She had no clue what his name was and she took this route all the time.

"Jack, you're going to push me off schedule again," the driver said grumpily.

"Come on, Carl, you know you can make up time on the next few stops." Jack ducked under the seat, found Lidia's jazz shoes, and handed them to her as she stood and watched. "No one gets off at those, right, gang?" He pointed to a woman knitting in the back row. "Cecilia? You're doing the whole loop today till you finish that baby blanket, aren't you? You're in no rush."

Everyone on the bus laughed.

How did he know everyone on this bus?

Jack dove under a seat again and came back seconds later with her dance bag. He smiled. "Here you go."

"Thanks," Lidia said, following him off the bus.

The two stared at each other at the bus stop. *What is he doing at Bradley?* Lidia wondered. He didn't go to school there—she knew everyone. It wasn't that big a school, but maybe he was starting in the fall.

"You're welcome," said Jack. Then he hopped back onto the bus! Lidia did a double take.

The driver groaned. "Jack! You're not even getting off?"

"Nope." Jack held on to the pole and winked at Lidia. "Just trying to save the day for Sailor Moon here." Lidia looked down at the small cartoon emblem on her dance bag. He knew who Sailor Moon was? "Have a great day!" he shouted as the doors closed almost on his nose.

Lidia smiled. She wasn't sure Jack had saved the day, but he'd definitely taken her mind off Sydney and Griffin.

For now.

CHAPTER FOUR

Julianna

"Uh oh, uh oh, uh oh, oh, no, no! Sing it with me, Julianna!" her mom yelled.

Julianna Ramirez covered her face with her hands. She knew what her mother was trying to do—loosen her up. But there was no loosening! They were three streetlights away from the start of her first day at her new high school, the Bradley Academy, and she was nervous.

More like petrified.

Julianna had gone to school with the same kids since kindergarten, and now she was entering the tenth grade at a new school, in a new town, that was almost two hours away from the city she would always call her home—Miami. With her mom's job transfer, her return address label would say "Naples, Florida." This did not sound as cool as Miami. She frowned as she thought of something else to worry about. She hoped her mom had made sure to forward all their mail. She was waiting to hear from a songwriting contest at that very moment.

Julianna grabbed several strands of her dark-brown hair and began to chew on them.

"*Uh oh, uh oh, uh oh, oh, no, no!*" Mrs. Ramirez sang again, off-key. She looked at Julianna expectantly. Julianna continued to chew on her hair. "Come on, Ju-Ju! 'Crazy in Love' is our song! You cannot dis Queen Bey by refusing to car jam with me!"

Her mother made the music louder as she pulled up to a light. She danced in her seat.

Her mother was crazy, but the beat was infectious. So were the lyrics. As much as she tried to ignore it, Beyoncé could not be ignored.

"*Got me looking so crazy right now! Your love's got me looking so crazy right now!*" she sang along with her mom, belting it for all she was worth.

By the end of their backup session for Beyoncé, Julianna was smiling. Then she realized they had turned into the Bradley Academy campus. That's right: *campus*.

After Julianna's mom found out her company was moving to Naples, they had taken a tour of Bradley and Julianna had been in awe. The place looked like her cousin Sofia's college in Boston that she was always posting pictures of. Bradley wasn't one building. There were several McMansions that held classrooms. In between the brick colonial buildings were turf fields and manicured lawns that looked like golf courses, state-of-the-art tech, science, and theater centers, plus an indoor pool with a retractable dome. Headmistress Sato, who gave them the tour personally, even lived on the campus with her family. Julianna wasn't sure how her mom was swinging the tuition, but her mom kept telling her not to worry. Her job transfer and promotion must have been big.

"You sounded lovely," her mom said, smiling at Julianna with a grin that was a mirror image of her own. They did have a *Gilmore Girls*–type relationship going on and they looked alike: same warm olive skin tone and chestnut-brown hair, same voice, and same stature (neither of them broke five four on the height chart). The key difference between them was that her mom had no problem singing in front of people and Julianna broke out in hives.

"Maybe you should join chorus here," her mom suggested.

"Mom," Julianna moaned. "Don't go there."

"I don't get this sudden fear of being in the spotlight!" her mother pressed. "Ever since you didn't make that Tonal Teens group, you've stopped singing anywhere people can hear you." She tsked. "So you had a bad audition. You try again!"

"I know," Julianna said tensely. "I just don't love to sing in front of people, okay? It has nothing to do with the Tonal Teens!"

Even though it kind of did. Ever since she had bombed her audition for her school's a cappella group—the award-winning, top five in the state, all-girls' a cappella group, the Tonal Teens—she had stopped singing anywhere but in her room or the shower. Julianna had taken the cut hard. She'd personally thought her cover of "Renegade" had been killer, but that just showed what she knew. Her best friend, Amy, had tried to console her.

"If you had made the Tonal Teens, then you wouldn't have started writing, and then you wouldn't be on your way to being a famous songwriter," Amy had said.

Amy had been the one who'd broken the bad news to Julianna about not making the team. Julianna was the only one of her friends who hadn't made the group, and she had taken it hard. That's when she'd started pouring her heart out in her diary. Soon, the entries turned to poetry and she found herself writing lyrics. Amy had loved one of her songs so much that the Tonal Teens had performed it last season and won first place in the competition. Encouraged, Julianna had started entering songwriting contests. She'd lost two that year already, so her track record wasn't good, but she was still waiting to hear from the Sounds of the Future high school songwriting contest. The deadline had been a month ago, which meant she should hear something any day.

"I still think the Tonal Teens were foolish to pass you up. I heard you practicing for auditions. You should have been named captain! Your abuela agrees with me!"

Julianna rolled her eyes. "Mom, Abuela also thinks I am going to be an Olympic beach volleyball player just because she saw me spike the ball over the net a few times."

"You *are* a good volleyball player," her mother said. Julianna couldn't help but smile. Her mom and abuela were 100 percent supportive even when Julianna's talents didn't really justify it.

Her mother drove through the school's gates to the drop-off area. "I'm sure if you try out for a singing group at Bradley, you'll get in."

"I think I'll stick with beach volleyball," Julianna teased. She was not putting herself out there like that ever again. It had been mortifying. She was sure there were plenty of things to do at Bradley that had nothing to do with music. Like archery (um, her aim was terrible)! Or sailing (she had grown up in Florida, but she couldn't say she was overly fond of being on a boat). Or gymnastics (if she could get over her irrational fear of heights). Hmm . . . academics it was!

"Good luck!" her mom said as Julianna stepped out of the car. "And let me know what time you want to be picked up. Or call if you end up with plans after school."

"I got it! You want me to make friends," Julianna said with a laugh. "I'll try!"

Even if I really miss my old ones. Back in Miami, Amy and Naya were starting classes too. It felt weird not to be with them, standing at the row of lockers they always decorated together. She heard her phone buzz.

NAYA: Good luck today! We miss you!

Naya had included a picture of herself and Amy. Julianna sent back a long string of heart emojis. Then it was time to face the music. She straightened her uniform's plaid jumper (it was kind of cute) and headed to Headmistress Sato's office. She'd asked to see Julianna before her first class, and the secretary ushered Julianna right inside. Headmistress Sato's office had a fireplace that was probably never used (this *was* southwest Florida). On the mantel behind Headmistress Sato's desk was a photo of her family that featured a young boy and a pretty girl Julianna's own age.

"Julianna, great to see you again." Headmistress Sato stood to greet her. "Welcome to Bradley!"

"Thank you." Julianna blushed slightly. She hated being the center of attention.

"Thanks for getting here early today. I wanted to go over the schedule you created online."

Julianna hoped she wasn't getting bounced from her elective pick, a music class called From Lennon to Kanye: How Artists Have Shaped the Music Industry. She'd been looking forward to that one more than any other class.

"It's regarding your music elective," Headmistress Sato said, pulling up the schedule on her laptop.

Great, Julianna thought. "I took Intro to Music at my old school."

"I know, and the elective you picked is fine."

Julianna breathed a sigh of relief.

"But it counts as one of your electives, not your music requirement," Headmistress Sato explained. "At Bradley, we believe arts are an important tool in broadening a student's horizon. That's why every student is required to participate in an extracurricular music program. You can choose from one of our choral groups, band, orchestra, wind ensemble, or marching band. Of course, you'll have to try out for the groups, but I'm sure we'll find you a spot in one of them." She smiled brightly.

Julianna's head started to spin. An extracurricular music program was something required of her in seventh grade, not tenth. "I love music," Julianna said slowly, "but like I mentioned at my entrance interview this summer, I'm more of a behind-the-scenes kind of girl. I love to write songs, not perform them." She had an idea. "Maybe I could write some music for one of the groups."

"If you write music, you must play music too, no?" Headmistress Sato pressed.

Darn. She had her there. "Yes. The piano and the guitar, but . . ."

Headmistress Sato perked up. "Wonderful! You can join the jazz band. Or maybe you want to work with our Rock Monsters, which is Bradley's very own rock group, which plays at the Bradley Café on select Friday nights throughout the school year."

Rock Monsters? She could not picture herself rocking out onstage or marching across the turf field with an instrument.

"I'm not really into rock," Julianna said. "I like to write show tunes. Like story songs for movie musicals? My goal is to one day be the next Kristen Anderson-Lopez." Headmistress Sato's expression was blank. "The Grammy-winning songwriter of *Frozen* who also co-created the Broadway show *In Transit?* I don't sing anymore."

"Anymore?" Oops. Headmistress Sato caught that part. "Why not? We have many choral groups you could try out for."

Julianna closed her eyes for a second and the image of Amy consoling her when she didn't make Tonal Teens popped into her head. "You could always join chorus," Amy had said. General chorus was the consolation prize. Anyone could join chorus at her old school, no tryouts necessary. There were, like, forty kids in it and the song selections were always traditional ("The Hallelujah Chorus") or had been sung to death (Pharrell Williams's "Happy"). She didn't want to be part of the chorus. "Are there any other options?"

Headmistress Sato's eyes lit up. "Our all-female a cappella group, the Nightingales, is excellent."

Julianna had put her foot in her mouth. "I meant other than choral or orchestra. I'm not good enough for a cappella." She looked down at her hands, which were clenched tight. "I didn't make the cut for a group at my old school."

"That doesn't mean you won't make the team here." Headmistress Sato sounded like Julianna's mother. "Bradley's all-girl a cappella group was once one of the most famed singing groups in southwest Florida." She frowned slightly. "But they've struggled the last few years and are looking for new talent. They almost didn't have enough girls to compete last year."

Julianna was curious. "Why not?"

Headmistress Sato's frown deepened. "Various mishaps, but the point is, they're looking for fresh talent. I was a founding member when I was a student here." She pointed to a yellowed photo of a group of girls wearing blue dress suits on her mantel. "You'd have to try out, of course, but my daughter is one of this year's co-captains. Why don't I message her and tell her you're coming to auditions after school today?"

"Today?" Julianna felt herself begin to perspire. She couldn't get up onstage and sing in front of new classmates today!

She could hear Amy's voice in her head again. "Ju-Ju, you didn't make the first cut."

Nope. No way. Absolutely not. She *wouldn't*. Her mom would have to find her a new school that didn't have crazy music requirements . . . even if she really liked the idea of this one.

She was not a Rock Monster.

She did not do jazz bands.

The thought of those silly marching band hats and the uncomfortable chin straps made her shudder.

An alarm went off on Headmistress Sato's desk. She shut it off and looked at Julianna. "Fifteen minutes until first period. So, we'll see you at the Nightingales auditions this afternoon?"

"I'm not sure . . . ," Julianna said apprehensively. "Is there a second tryout day, because I told my mom to pick me up today at four and . . ."

The headmistress was already on her phone, clearly sending a message to her daughter. "Great!" she said as if she hadn't heard Julianna. "You're all set. They'll be expecting you."

Julianna was going to be ill. "Oh, I, well, I hope my mom can . . ." Headmistress Sato's phone was ringing. Julianna took that as her cue to exit.

As she left the building, she could see the campus coming alive. There were dozens of students walking to various buildings. Every few seconds someone would scream and run into another uniform-clad girl's arms, or two guys would high-five and start trading summer stories. Julianna kept her head down and tried not to let her panic about the afternoon's auditions take over. If she did, she'd soon be under a palm tree rocking back and forth.

Whenever Julianna thought of singing in front of people now, her hands became clammy and she got a chalky taste in her mouth. She could feel her heart start to zoom and there was a rushing sound like wind in her ears. Her instinct was always to run, hide, disappear. She told herself she was being ridiculous—people got rejected from things every day. It was one audition. But it had been a big one. She'd wanted to be in the Tonal Teens since she and Amy saw them perform during a spring concert when they were in sixth grade. Amy had gotten in. Julianna hadn't. Was she foolish to think her voice was decent? Naya had said Julianna's audition was excellent and she was a "sure thing." How could she get passed over for Margot Bishop, who couldn't even match keys?

BA-BA-BA-BUMP! THUMP! CLANG!

People stopped talking and were looking around to see where the sound had come from. It sounded like drums, but there was no sign of a concert going on in the quad and she didn't see any sound systems outside. Maybe they played music at Bradley between classes?

"Bradley Academy! Gooooood morning!"

Around her, girls started to scream and run in the direction of the voice.

Julianna felt herself get carried along with the crowd toward a building with a balcony where a bunch of guys were standing.

A boy wearing silver shades and a uniform blazer jumped up on a chair with a microphone in his hand. "How you doing, Bradley?" he shouted. "I'm co-captain Dave Wallace, and we are the a cappella champions the Kingfishers!" Everyone in the crowd below started to cheer. "No first-day-of-school frowns this morning," Dave continued as the guys behind him started to *ooh* and *aah*. "We are going to make you smile!"

"If you want to hear good a cappella, come listen to us," said another guy, "not the Nightingales." A few people laughed. Others booed.

The Nightingales. Julianna frowned. That was the group she was supposed to try out for, wasn't it? She looked at her phone. If she didn't get moving, she'd be late to class, but now people had filled in around her and she was boxed in. "Excuse me," she said, trying to squeeze out of the crowd. No one was moving.

"Now, now." Dave calmed the boos. "The Nightingales were good—ten years ago." More laughs. "But we're excellent. So if you're a guy out there who wants to join an a cappella group that you don't have to be ashamed of, try out for the Kingfishers today!"

Julianna cringed.

"And to prove how good we are, we're going to kick off your first day back with a song," said a tall kid with spiky blue hair.

The cheers intensified as the guys ran down the balcony steps and came to where the crowd was gathered. Julianna tried to make a break for it, but instead found herself pushed to the front in time to see a heavyset guy start beatboxing the tune of "Happy." (She rolled her eyes.) The rest of the Kingfishers adjusted the mics on their headsets, then began to sing the familiar tune. A pale blond with hazel eyes stepped to the front.

"Hold up!" he said.

"What is it, Griffin?" Dave asked as the rest of the guys appeared to look baffled.

"Since when do we just sing one song?" Griffin asked with a sly smile. "We're Kingfishers. Let's layer another tune in here and make things interesting."

Griffin started to sing "Come On Get Happy," a song Julianna vaguely knew from some old TV show. Then "Happy" came in again and the two songs were being sung simultaneously by different parts, the harmonies layering over one another and merging.

It sounded so good, for a moment Julianna forgot she was still standing there.

"Audience participation time!" Griffin shouted. "Let's give a girl a rare chance to be a Kingfisher!"

Before Julianna knew what was happening, Griffin had run out into the crowd. He shoved a microphone in Julianna's face. She thought she was going to pass out.

"It's your turn!" Griffin said as the other guys kept the harmony going. "Sing it!"

CHAPTER FIVE

Lidia

Oh no, they didn't!

From her backyard, Lidia could hear cheering, singing, and beatboxing. Were the Kingfishers really breaking the rules already and hosting a first-day-of-school concert?

They'd promised they wouldn't! Lidia had seen the email from Mr. Wickey himself asking both groups to tone down the pranking this season. They were also asked to avoid any performances till after auditions. Now the guys were singing in front of the whole school?

Not if Lidia had anything to say about it!

She ran across the grass, holding on to her backpack to keep it from falling off. She could see the crowd gathered in front of the cafeteria cheering. Lidia could picture smug Dave saying something obnoxious, like: *"This is your chance to be part of a team destined for a cappella glory. Five-times-in-a-row state champions, the Kingfishers, will be holding auditions this afternoon! And, um, girls,* the Nightingales are hosting their auditions today, but no one wants to be one of them!"

She could hear the guys singing "Happy" as she got closer. *They couldn't think of something more original to sing?* she thought. Then she heard another tune being sung at the same time. One she'd never imagined the Kingfishers knowing. Was that the theme to *The Partridge Family*?

Lidia stopped short when she neared the front of the crowd and saw Griffin. Just the sight of him made Lidia feel like fireworks were about to erupt over her head. She watched him hold out a microphone to a girl in the crowd. Lidia's stomach tightened. Was the girl Sydney? Lidia moved closer to see.

It wasn't Sydney. It was a girl she didn't recognize and she looked like a deer caught in headlights. Lidia couldn't blame her. Griffin had that effect on people.

"Sing!" Griffin told her, holding on to the microphone so many girls were clamoring for. Then he gave the girl the smile that always made her fall for him all over again.

There was just so much to love about Griffin Mancini. From the small gap between his two front lower teeth to his hazel eyes that made him screensaver-worthy (literally, a picture of Griffin with the Kingfishers was her secret screensaver). Then there was the I-just-stepped-out-of-a-1950s-movie blond hair, which he usually swept to the side in a wave.

"I . . . ," the girl stuttered. The crowd's cheering started to wane. "I . . ."

"Sing!" someone in the crowd shouted.

"Grif, move on to a new girl," one of the Kingfishers rudely shouted.

The girl just stood there. Lidia felt bad for her. This girl, who was obviously new, was being thrust into the spotlight and she clearly wasn't ready. Someone had to save her. Lidia didn't want that someone to be Sydney, who was probably in the crowd just waiting for her chance to sing with Griffin. Sydney had sung with Griffin all summer. It was Lidia's turn.

She marched up to Griffin and put her hand over his on the mic. Then she looked at the girl. "Do you mind if I jump in?"

The girl looked grateful. "Take it," she said and quickly dipped back into the crowd.

Lidia looked questioningly at Griffin. "Go for it, Sato," he said.

That was all the encouragement she needed. She sang *The Partridge Family* tune Grandma Evie had drilled into her head for years. *"Hello world, there's a song that we're singing . . ."*

Griffin joined her. *"Come on get happy!"*

The crowd cheered again and Lidia's heart beat in double-time. She was singing with Griffin Mancini in front of the whole school!

The rest of the school faded away and all Lidia could see was her and Griffin. He stared straight into her eyes the way she'd always imagined and she held his gaze. Maybe she wasn't as bad at this boy thing as she thought she was. Other than Dougie, she hadn't had much practice talking to the opposite sex. She'd never had a real boyfriend before—if she discounted Michael, that guy who walked her to her locker every day for three months in eighth grade—or even a good male friend. It had just always been easier for her to fantasize about talking to guys than actually doing it. But now she was singing with a boy, so that was a major improvement.

They came to the last line of the song. *"Come on get happy!"* Lidia and Griffin sang in harmony. Griffin threw an arm around her and Lidia practically squeaked.

"The Kingfishers aren't the only ones hosting auditions today," she said, composing herself. "Try out for the new and improved Nightingales. We're going to take the competition by storm this season—and that includes these guys." Lidia pointed to Griffin, who pretended to look wounded. "Don't let them fool you. You definitely don't want to miss out on a group this amazing!" The crowd cheered. She'd done her group proud.

Griffin held out his hand. "That mic is Kingfishers' property, so I'll need to take it back before you tamper with it."

If he only knew the Nightingales had already tampered with the guys' traditional auditions pizza order. *Hope you like the taste of anchovies!* Lidia thought. Sydney had texted Lidia to say she'd made the order after the jelly beans fiasco. Lidia read the text, but hadn't responded. She was secretly glad Sydney had pulled the prank, though.

Lidia gave him the mic. "You guys aren't scared of a group of girls, are you?"

Griffin stepped closer. "I wouldn't be if I knew what you guys had up your sleeve."

The words were on the tip of Lidia's tongue. *I've liked you for years and never told you and now I'm worried it's too late.* Instead, Lidia laughed and it came out more like a mouse squeak. "You'll see soon enough," she said.

"I'll see you at auditions," Griffin said.

Auditions meant she, Griffin, and Sydney were going to be in the same room.

She may have been avoiding Sydney's calls and texts, but that afternoon she was going to have to face the music. Literally and figuratively. "See you there," Lidia said and watched him walk away. She heard her phone ping. She had several texts. The first was from Sydney.

SYDNEY: Hate when we don't talk! Meet me in the quad before auditions? Please?

SYDNEY: If you don't, I will take over the Bradley Academy loudspeaker system and dedicate Kenny Rogers's "Through the Years" to you and sing it at the top of my lungs.

SYDNEY: Don't test me. You know I'll do it.

Lidia had to bite her lip to keep from laughing. Sydney *would* make good on her promise if Lidia didn't show. The Kenny Rogers tune was Syd's grandparents' wedding song and the girls' cheesy friendship anthem. Lidia hated fighting, especially with her best friend. Nightingales auditions would go up in flames if the two of them fought that afternoon. Lidia winced when she thought of the things she'd said in front of the other girls at Pinocchio's. She did not want the world knowing what was going on with them or about her crush on Griffin. It was time she got this conversation over with. She wrote Sydney back: Fountain 3 p.m.

Then she read her other text. It was from a number she didn't recognize.

> Hi, Lidia! It's Miss Pattie Ann at Integral Dance Arts. Are you taking class today? If so, can we chat? There is something I want to discuss with you. How is 4 p.m.?

Miss Pattie Ann was her favorite dance instructor. Maybe she was going to let Lidia move into a more advanced class. Lidia was dying to know, but she'd be at Nightingales auditions till around five. Reluctantly, she texted Miss Pattie Ann that she wouldn't be in till tomorrow. The school tower bell chimed, warning Lidia she had three minutes to get to her first class. She picked up the backpack she had thrown down before her song session.

Singing with Griffin, a talk with Syd, and a text from Miss Pattie Ann. The first day of school was turning out to be way more interesting than she thought it would be and it was only getting started.

CHAPTER SIX

Sydney

It was a weird feeling watching your best friend and the boy you weren't supposed to like—but definitely did—talking.

Sydney's bus driver had gotten lost on their route trying to find a new student's address, and they'd pulled up to campus ten minutes before the first bell. Sydney had hoped to be there earlier to hand out flyers for the Nightingales' auditions. Instead she found an elated Lidia dueting with He Who Shall Not Be Named in front of half of Bradley Academy.

It was the moment Sydney had wanted Lidia to have with him for forever, and yet, seeing it play out in front of her, Sydney felt like she was having an out-of-body experience. Part of her screamed, *Go, Lid!* while the other part yelled, *He's mine!* But he wasn't. *This is the way it's supposed to be*, she told herself, but she didn't stick around to see if they did an encore. Instead, she walked to class and texted Lidia, asking her to meet before auditions.

Now it was almost three p.m. and Sydney was pacing back and

forth in front of their favorite bench, the one that faced the dolphin fountain. She had no clue what she was going to say to Lidia. The words "I'm sorry" didn't feel like enough. Buying Lidia her favorite chocolate nonpareils, balloons, or cute flip-flops didn't feel right either.

Maybe she should let Lidia hit her. Hard. That might make her feel better.

Sydney winced at the thought. She cried when she got a splinter. She couldn't imagine a sock to the jaw.

Lidia arrived before Sydney had a chance to figure it out.

"Hi," Lidia said shyly. Her face looked as anxious as Sydney felt.

"Hi!" Sydney said, hovering near their bench, like she was afraid to move. "Thanks for coming. I saw you singing with Griffin this morning. Yay you!" *God, that sounded fake.*

Lidia looked at the ground. "Should we talk? We have to get to auditions."

"Yes," Sydney said, patting the bench. "Let's talk."

They stared at each other and quickly sat down.

It was awkwardly quiet. All Sydney could hear was the fountain gurgling. After practice one day last spring, the team had jumped into it and splashed around till a security guard at school yelled at them to get out. Today would not be one of those days. She guessed she needed to go first.

"You were kind of harsh at Pinocchio's the other day," Sydney said, immediately realizing it was the wrong thing to say when she saw Lidia's eyes narrow.

"I was harsh?" Lidia sputtered.

"No, I mean, yes, but it's just that I know you were mad at me," Sydney backpedaled, "and you had a right to be, but to tell everyone your side of the story made me look bad." Lidia's mouth fell open. This was not going well at all. "I just mean, I wanted to explain everything to you first. Not have every prospective Nightingale hear us air our dirty laundry. People were so upset about what happened, several left right after you stormed out. I think we lost some good candidates because of what was said."

Sydney could see the veins bulging in Lidia's neck. "So now you're blaming this whole thing on me?" Lidia asked.

Okay, maybe that hadn't been the right thing to say either. Sydney was so bad at this sort of thing. She hated debate class and oral presentations because she could never put her thoughts into words. It was easier to read song lyrics. If someone told her what to say, she would nail it. She was not good at improv. "No! I just wanted you to know that, I mean, I thought you should know that I . . . it wasn't . . . he didn't . . . . I mean, I didn't . . . I . . ."

Lidia crossed her arms. "We're going to be late for auditions if you don't say what you actually want to say."

Ouch! Did she have to be so mean? She had a right to be furious, but it still hurt to be the one Lidia was mad at. Fighting with Lidia was the absolute worst. Why couldn't she find the words to apologize with? She needed a script! Oh! That gave her an idea. Her breathing slowed and she tried to focus.

"I know anything I say isn't enough," Sydney began, her

confidence returning. She adjusted her glittery green headband (it reminded her of *Wicked*). "I could say 'I'm sorry' over and over a thousand times a day for a thousand years and it wouldn't change what I did. I'd step into a time machine and go back in time if I could. I'd find a genie and rub his magic lamp to get out of this moment. I'd wish upon a million stars too, but maybe it's better I always remember what happened. I should live with the guilt every day so that I never hurt you that way again." She smiled tentatively.

Lidia blinked at her. "Did you really just recite that scene from *Do Over* to me? The one where Samantha apologizes to Jillian? Did you think I wouldn't know it?"

Idiot! Of course, Lidia would know that scene. They both loved that movie.

Sydney held up her right hand. "Guilty." Lidia slapped her hand to her forehead and started walking away. "I'm sorry, okay? You know I'm bad at this sort of thing! I screwed up! Badly!" Her lower lip quivered. She just wanted to forget this whole thing had ever happened. "But I didn't mean it!" Lidia was circling the fountain now. "It's not even my fault! If you had stayed and seen what really happened, you'd know it was no big deal."

Lidia did a double take.

"He kissed me. I did not kiss him back. I pushed him away, but you were probably gone by that point."

Lidia just looked at her.

"I'm serious." Sydney tried again. "I think he was just wrapped up in the moment because we'd just done our last *In the Heights* performance the night before. We put so much time into that performance, maybe he was just trying to thank me for acting, um, so actorly and professional as his co-star." Sydney suddenly felt very hot.

"Syd," Lidia said dryly. "You've got to be kidding me."

"No!" Sydney was floundering, but an actress always embraced her scene. "You were the one who asked me to get close to him so I could talk you up. That's what I did."

Lidia's face reddened. "I didn't mean *that* close!"

She'd put her foot into her mouth again. "I know, but I wouldn't have started spending so much time with him if you hadn't asked me to." Lidia grunted. "But again, the kiss was his fault. Not mine."

"His fault?" Lidia repeated.

"Yes." Sydney nodded vigorously. Maybe she was finally getting through to her. They had a common enemy: Griffin! "When I walked in to Don't Be Crabby's early, it was to snag a table for us. I wasn't expecting to see Griffin or be kissed! If he had said something about liking me, I could have stopped him, you know? He caught me completely off-guard. To do that in public, where you could walk in at any moment and *did* walk in? What a jerk!" She put a hand on Lidia's arm. "You could do so much better than a guy like Griffin. We are going to find you someone much cuter and sweeter." She waited a beat. "So, are we good?"

"Are you serious right now?" Lidia repeated.

"You're still upset, I get it," Sydney said, "but could we put all of this aside at auditions? I don't want to lose anyone else, and if people think we're still fighting, it could be off-putting." Lidia loved the Nightingales as much as she did. She'd see that putting the auditions first was the right thing to do.

"See you at auditions," Lidia said flatly and walked away.

Sydney exhaled. "Okay. See you in a few!"

That didn't go so badly after all. They were going to be okay. Who needed Griffin Mancini? Syd closed her eyes for a moment and saw his face. She could picture Griffin running lines with her at the playhouse. Bringing her passion fruit tea (her favorite) when she'd lost her voice, and leaving a protein bar on her playbook because he knew she always forgot to eat when she was rehearsing.

He was a good guy, but what kind of guy just kisses a girl in the middle of a coffee shop when she asks him if he can pass the sweetener? Lidia could do much better than a guy like Griffin. They both could!

"Hey, Syd," Griffin said, appearing in front of her.

Sydney screamed and pushed him as hard as she could. Griffin went stumbling back and landed in a patch of grass. Ooh. That was definitely going to leave a grass stain.

"What did you do that for?" Griffin asked, quickly jumping up, his face flushed, as he stood too close for comfort. How could a boy look that cute in a cheesy Kingfishers tee with a giant striped bass on the front that said IT'S GOOD TO BE KING? Did he have to smell good too? The coconut aroma he was giving off mixed with Dove soap was dizzying.

The scent reminded her of the kiss that never should have happened. She didn't want to smell coconut. And she really didn't want to think about that perfect kiss.

One minute they had been laughing about her use of way too much sweetener, the next he had been wiping the chocolate syrup from her coffee drink off her mouth and they were kissing. His mouth was sweet, his lips softer than she'd imagined, and he smelled even better.

She closed her eyes to block out the shameful memory. She had betrayed her best friend and she hated herself for it. She hated Griffin for it! She pushed Griffin again.

"Ow! Syd, what is going on?" Griffin asked.

"You ruined everything!" Sydney almost cried. "Lidia is so mad at me!"

"Lidia's mad? Why?" Griffin looked really confused.

Oops. He didn't know about Lidia's crush. She may have gotten close to him that summer for Lidia, but now that she thought about it, she'd never once even hinted that Lidia liked him. Why hadn't she told him? Maybe then this story would have played out differently.

Syd pushed her hair behind her ears. "Because you guys pranked us, of course. We were trying to recruit new members and now your jelly bean prank ruined everything."

"About that," Griffin said, following Sydney as she went to grab her book bag by the fountain. "Dave just got a pizza delivery for auditions and the pies are covered in anchovies. He's not too happy. You guys might want to watch your step at auditions today."

"Why? Are you pranking us back?" Sydney pressed.

"Did I say the word 'prank'? I don't think I used that word." Griffin's eyes were full of mischief. "Pranks on audition days aren't allowed, which is why I'm *sure* you guys had nothing to do with the pizza à la anchovies."

"Absolutely not." Sydney folded her arms. "We would never stoop to the Kingfishers' level."

Griffin smirked. "Great. No need to start off the season with either group getting in trouble. This is supposed to be fun."

"Exactly," Sydney agreed. That's what sophomore year was supposed to be. No SAT worries or college talk yet. All she had to worry about was her a cappella group. That meant there was no time for boys. Sydney and Lidia had to take the Nightingales from worst in south Florida to first, and that started with auditions. She looked at her fitness tracker, which doubled as a clock. She had to get going.

What if it was already standing room only? Maybe there would be so many girls they'd have to hold auditions two days in a row. She could just picture the Kingfishers' smug smiles fading as they saw who Bradley was really embracing this year—the Nightingales! It was going to be a great season and she just wanted to get started.

"The Nightingales don't have time for major pranks this year anyway," she said, heading to the arts center. Griffin followed. "If we score well at the Turn It Up competition in November, that will get us into the Panhandle Pump It Up, and then if we get in the top three there we'll be on to the Daytona Word of Mouth and . . ."

Griffin stepped in front of her. "Are you saying you have no time for me? I hope not."

Griffin was standing so close she could grab a fistful of his T-shirt. She stared at the cartoon bass on the front. "No time. I'm very dedicated to my craft this year and only my craft. I've got no time for anything or anyone else."

He stepped closer. His eyes begged to be looked at. "Even me?"

His breath was minty and he looked so good. Why did he have to stand so close? He should be standing that close to Lidia like he was that morning. He was hers for the taking if Lidia still wanted him. "I have to go." Sydney pushed past him.

"Remember what I said," he called after her. "Watch your step! It's the only warning you'll get from me this year if you have no time to talk."

"I don't need your help!" Sydney stomped past the fountain, sending a few birds flying. She clutched her Nightingales audition notes and scales to her chest. She repeated the words over and over again, hoping they'd stick: *Griffin who?*

CHAPTER SEVEN

Lidia

That was what Sydney was worried about? How their fight would look to girls auditioning for the Nightingales?

What about the fact that she had kissed the boy Lidia had liked since eighth grade?

Lidia was fuming—*fuming!*—as she speed walked away from Sydney and headed to the theater for auditions. Classmates moved out of the way when they saw her stony expression.

Her talk with Sydney hadn't made things better. It had made things worse! She knew Sydney tended to get tunnel vision—she'd get so wrapped up in a project she couldn't think of anything but the prize—but this was their friendship. Sydney was like the sister she didn't have. Their relationship was sacred, or at least it was supposed to be. How could Sydney not see how wrong she had been to hide this from her? Maybe the kiss with Griffin had been a mistake, but if it was, why couldn't Sydney have been truthful?

Hot tears plopped down Lidia's cheeks. She quickly wiped them away before anyone could see. She felt like a fool. Her best friend had traded her in for the boy she liked. Did Griffin know how Lidia felt? He hadn't said anything that morning. Would he say something that afternoon at auditions?

Lidia stopped short and took deep breaths. She knew she couldn't face them both that afternoon, but what choice did she have? She couldn't just not show up at her own team's auditions.

"Hey, Lidia! Something wrong?"

Lidia spun around, wiping her eyes again as she spotted the two girls walking toward her. *Great.* Of all the people she could run into, it had to be Whitney Corcoran and Micayla Reves.

When Mr. Wickey had put out the call for potential new captains, it had been Whitney and Micayla who had campaigned against them. Things had gotten ugly quickly, with Whitney and Micayla trying to convince other Nightingales not to vote for Lidia and Sydney, but in the end, she and Syd had won anyway. Whitney and Micayla had been bitter ever since. Lidia wasn't even sure they'd come back to the team this year, but here they were on their way to auditions.

"Hi, guys." Lidia forced a smile. "How was your summer?"

"Amazing!" Whitney was sporting a deep summer tan that accentuated the gold in her highlighted hair, which hung in perfect waves down her back. "I was accepted into a musical theater program run by the University of Florida. Way more fulfilling than what I could have been doing in community theater. No offense."

That was a dig at Sydney. "No offense taken." Lidia played it cool. She'd seen their thinly veiled social media comments about a certain team making the biggest mistake of their lives and how the group wouldn't survive the year.

"And I recorded a demo in New York," Micayla added. She was equally stylish with her hair in short curls and her body toned from summer soccer practices. That was the only activity that she did without Whitney. The two were inseparable, much like Lidia and Syd had been before Griffingate. "Nothing's happened yet, but my agent is talking to all the right people. He says my demo has a lot of buzz, so I may have to leave for New York for meetings any day now."

Lidia made a sad face. "Sounds like you guys are too busy to be Nightingales this year."

"Oh no," Whitney said quickly. "We're trying out. That poor team needs some actual talent, don't you think? No offense."

"None taken," Lidia said again, digging her nails into her own arm.

"We heard all about the drama at Pinocchio's last week, though," Whitney said. "Sorry we had to miss it. I was getting a Rising Star award for my college program."

"And I was in New York," Micayla added.

"So you mentioned," Lidia said.

"But wow! Lidia! I had no idea you had such a temper!" Whitney nudged her. "Blowing up at Sydney in front of all those new recruits? I hope some of those girls forgive you and show up today. If not, we won't have a team."

"Whit, don't be harsh. Lidia was betrayed by her best friend." Micayla linked arms with an unwilling Lidia and looked at her sadly. "Everyone knows you've liked Griffin Mancini forever and a day."

Lidia stopped short. "They do?"

Whitney looked somewhat sympathetic. "It's kind of obvious. How could Sydney do that to you? And now you have to face the two of them together at auditions?" Whitney looked toward the theater. "I wouldn't want to go in there if I were you. You're so brave."

"So brave," Micayla repeated.

For a split second, Lidia actually thought, *Sydney, where are you?* "It's no big deal," Lidia forced herself to say. *It was.* "We're fine." *We're not.* "And we've been prepping for auditions all summer. A little fight can't stop us from taking this team to the top again. I hope you brought your A game for auditions." Sure, them getting back on the team was almost certain—they were good singers—but it was fun to watch them squirm.

"Of course," Whitney said. "Not that we needed much prep work. I'm sure us getting on the team is a lock." Whitney looked at Micayla. "We're just glad to hear you guys are fine. This team can't function without two captains. It's how all the a cappella groups have always run." She made a sad face. "I'd hate to see one of you drop out and someone else have to jump in midseason."

Lidia's stomach lurched. "That won't be a problem. Sydney and I are fine."

They weren't fine, but she hoped she could be as good an actress as Sydney and pretend to be. Auditions were only two hours. They could survive sitting next to each other for two hours.

Couldn't they?

CHAPTER EIGHT

Julianna

When Julianna entered the Performing Arts Center that afternoon, she was prepared to hear girls whisper about her. *That girl is trying out? Didn't she choke in front of the mic this morning?* Instead, she found herself standing in a packed lobby full of . . . boys.

Huh?

Julianna looked down at her notebook where she had scribbled the audition time for the Nightingales. *3 p.m.!* she had written. And crossed it out. And written again. All day she was at war with herself about auditions. If she couldn't handle an impromptu karaoke session on the lawn, how was she going to stand up in front of her new classmates and sing by herself?

Remember: the tuba, she told herself. *You don't want to learn to play it or be a Rock Monster. You have to try out, Julianna!* She would ask someone where the Nightingales were auditioning and she would force herself to go there. Right now. Any second. *Just take a step forward, Julianna.*

She took a step forward and THUMP! Her legs went flying out from under her.

Julianna slid on the shiny, sticky floor, right into a group of boys, her arms waving wildly as she reached out to grab one of their jackets and hang on for dear life rather than fall in all that goop. Her mind raced in the three seconds from slip to impact. Was that maple syrup? It smelled divine, but it was all over her shoes, which were now sticking to the floors. Gross!

She grabbed for a guy and missed—landing on the floor instead.

The boys around her all started to cheer and whistle.

"And just like that, the first Nightingale slides into last place!" yelled Dave, the guy she remembered from this morning.

Okay, she was going to fall into the floor and disappear now. Thank you.

Someone knocked Dave out of the way.

"What's wrong with you guys?" a girl yelled, grabbing Julianna by the arm and yanking her up. "Pranks at auditions are against the rules! And now it smells like syrup in here!"

It was the girl who had saved her from the mic that morning.

Dave smirked. "You're right. They are, which is why we're wondering how our pizzas arrived this afternoon covered with anchovies."

The girl blinked. "Wasn't me." She turned to Julianna. "Let's dry you off before auditions." She helped her gingerly step around the maple syrup spill. "Everyone watch your step! Everyone . . . hey . . . where are the girls?" Lidia turned around to glare at Dave again. "Where did you send all the girls auditioning?" she demanded.

Dave laughed. "There aren't any! We didn't even need to prank you guys. You pranked yourselves. You've got no one trying out!" The guys all laughed.

She pulled Julianna away. "Ignore him. He's the Kingfishers' captain, first bass, and resident prank leader. He's also a jerk. The girls have to be here somewhere." She headed toward another set of double doors. "I'm Lidia Sato, by the way."

"Julianna Ramirez," she said, wiping the syrup on her skirt before she shook Lidia's hand.

"You're new, right?" Lidia's eyes widened. "Hey. You're the girl from this morning! The one I stole the mic from at the sing-along."

"Guilty as charged," Julianna said, her blood pumping. "Thanks for rescuing me. It's not that I didn't want to sing," she babbled. "I love singing. It's just that it's my first day and one minute I was looking for the science center and the next I was being handed a microphone and I didn't know the song and . . ."

Lidia held up her hand to stop her. "No need to explain. The Kingfishers drive me mad too. The Kingfishers weren't even supposed to be recruiting this morning." She pulled open the double doors. Lidia looked suddenly relieved. "There *are* girls here. Thank God."

Inside the theater there were at least a dozen girls in uniform standing near the stage. Definitely not as many girls as boys, but at least Julianna wasn't alone.

"Lidia! Lidia! Over here!" A high-strung, skinny girl marched over, sunglasses on even though they were indoors. "Don't tell me they got you! We all came around the back of the theater because we were sure the Kingfishers were up to something." The girl suddenly noticed Julianna and pointed to her. "Who's this? And why does she smell like maple syrup?"

"Gabby," Lidia said, "meet Julianna. She's new and trying out for the Nightingales. And the Kingfishers coated the floor with syrup and now the lobby is a mess."

"The custodians are going to be furious with them. Yay!" Gabby hugged Julianna. "And yay to new blood! Thank the a cappella gods! I was worried there weren't enough of us trying out. Then the group would be disbanded and I'd have to be in the general chorus or my mom would make me play the clarinet again and . . ." A girl next to her poked her in the ribs. "I mean, yay! More Nightingales auditioners!"

"Can you guys find Julianna a towel or something while I find Mr. Wickey to go over auditions?" Lidia asked.

"Of course." Gabby grabbed Julianna and brought her backstage. "I'm Gabby and this is Viola, and I'll show you around, and . . . Ah, a towel!" She tossed the towel hanging on a rack backstage to Julianna. "The curse hasn't struck again."

"Gabs, there is no curse!" Viola said, removing her purple headphones from her ears. She tossed a few pieces of gum into her mouth and began to chew. "You can call me Vi. This is the first year Gabs and I are trying out. I finally convinced Gabby to audition with me."

"I've been afraid of the curse," Gabby said and Viola rolled her eyes. "It's true! The curse is what caused Lidia to freak out on Sydney

71

last week at that Nightingales meeting at Pinocchio's." She looked at Julianna. "Lidia and Sydney are captains. They've wanted to run the group since they were in the Bradley lower school, before the team took a nosedive. To want to take over a team that was bombing every show they performed in is dedication."

"Gabs!" Vi groaned, rubbing her temples. Music was still playing from her headphones and Julianna could hear it. "Stop making Julianna second-guess herself. We can't afford to lose anyone auditioning or there won't even be a team to be part of."

Julianna's mouth suddenly felt dry. "Why do you think the group is cursed?" she asked, trying to think of anything but that large, shiny, bright stage that was just feet away. Girls were now walking on it willingly! She could hear them practicing their audition pieces and running scales. Julianna hadn't practiced anything. She still remembered her audition piece from the Tonal Teens, though. Was she really going to tempt fate and try that song again?

Gabby counted on her fingers. "One, two, three, four! Think about it! The last few years they've lost championships, had team-wide food poisoning, had members fall off the stage, and now the new captains are fighting over a boy." She leaned in to whisper in Julianna's ear. "Bad luck follows this group." Viola nudged Gabby and Gabby attempted an awkward smile. "But don't worry. Viola says the Nightingales are just having a rough patch, and Lidia and Sydney can turn it around. My family runs a doggy day care business, and when the dogs in Doggone It! This Dog Needs a Day Out! fight, they get over it eventually." Gabby smiled. "Lidia and Syd will too."

Julianna nodded as she continued to dab the sticky syrup with the towel. She was a mess. Was she really going to audition like this? Bad luck had already found her.

"Gabs tends to overreact," Viola told Julianna.

"I do not!" Gabby barked. "Okay, maybe I do."

Viola motioned to a man in a sweater vest. "Look. Sydney and Lidia are talking to Mr. Wickey, the club advisor, right now. They're not fighting."

The auditorium doors opened and the Kingfishers came strolling in loudly. Mr. Wickey tried to get their attention. "Calm down, everyone. Let's get started."

"Come on," Gabby said, grabbing Julianna's arm before she could change her mind. "Let's get backstage and warm up." Gabby led them to a spot backstage where they could see the captains in the audience and the people auditioning.

A short while later, after the club advisor had gone over the audition process, Julianna heard the first girl called to the stage.

"Mercedes Benz?"

Some of the guys in the audience snickered.

A tall girl with straight, light-brown hair that gave her at least another two inches of height glared at the audience. "Who wouldn't want to be named after the classiest car in the world, which my daddy bought me for my first car, by the way. How many of you guys have a Benz?" The guys shut up fast. "That's what I thought." She had such confidence that Julianna was in awe. They watched Mercedes as she stopped center stage, quickly ran through the exercises with Mr. Wickey, and started to sing "Defying Gravity" from *Wicked*.

"SOMETHING HAS CHANGED WITHIN ME," Mercedes sang at the top of her lungs.

Gabby, Viola, and Julianna held their ears. In the audience, Julianna saw the co-captains wince and write something down in their notebooks. They whispered to each other heatedly.

"Whoa! She's loud, but I think she's got a fifty-fifty shot," Gabby said. "They need warm bodies."

"Gabby and Viola, hey," said a pretty girl with long, golden hair. The girl with her, who had short, curly hair, struck the same hand-on-hip pose. They both looked the girls up and down. "Didn't know you were trying out. Fun. Who's this? And why are you all wet?"

"She fell victim to a Kingfishers' prank," Gabby explained. "Syrup on the floor."

"Oh." Both girls nodded, but neither seemed sympathetic.

"If we were captains, there would be no more pranks," said the first girl. She smiled at Julianna. "I'm Whitney and this is Micayla. We were up for captains this year, but lost by a handful of votes. Like two." Something about the girl's attitude reminded Julianna of her best friend, Amy.

"If the voting was done at the beginning of the a cappella season, we'd definitely be the ones holding auditions right now," said Micayla. "I just cut a demo in New York so I can spot talent easily."

"So can I," said Whitney. "I was accepted into a college musical theater program this past summer."

"But you still lost," Viola said bluntly, placing her head-phones back on her head. "So I guess we all have to impress Lidia and Sydney today."

"Guess so," Whitney said stiffly. "Till they start fighting again and leave the group hanging. Then we'll be there to pick up the pieces." Her smile was slick. "Good luck, girls." The two walked off.

"I can't stand them," Gabby said under her breath. "They think they're the next Taylor Swift."

"Lidia and Sydney are better," Viola said, bopping along to the music in her ears. "Maybe there will be so much talent here they won't even make the cut."

Make the cut. Amy's voice broke into her thoughts again. "You didn't make the first cut," she heard Amy say. Julianna started to sweat. What was she doing here? She wasn't going to make this group.

"Pearl Robbins?" Mr. Wickey called.

"Oh, Pearl." Viola tsked. "I heard she tried out last year and was really pitchy."

"Maybe she's gotten better," Gabby said hopefully as they all turned their eyes to the stage.

Pearl took the stage and launched into the same song from *Wicked* as Mercedes. Seemed like everyone was sticking with *Wicked*. Some words sounded great, but others were way out of tune. *"SomeTHING has ChanGED withIN ME . . ."*

Julianna looked to the audience. The Kingfishers in the auditorium laughed, but Lidia and Sydney barely raised an eyebrow as they wrote their notes.

What will they write in their notebooks when I try out? Julianna thought. *Nothing! You're not Pearl. You know you can sing. You just had a bad Tonal Teens audition.*

Girl Number Three strolled onstage with a stack of red Solo cups and everyone backstage groaned. As Julianna suspected, the girl took a seat on the stage, sat cross-legged, and broke into Anna Kendrick's "Cups" from *Pitch Perfect*.

Gabby shook her head. "That's an a cappella no-no."

"You never do *Pitch Perfect* music at an a cappella audition," Vi agreed. "Everyone knows that."

"Viola Chasez?" Mr. Wickey called two minutes later.

"That's me!" Viola said, removing her headphones again. She took a deep breath. "Wish me luck!"

Viola took the stage without any hesitation, handed her sheet music to the piano player, and launched into *Hamilton*'s "Satisfied." By the time she started rapping, the entire backstage was leaning onstage to hear Viola's soulful voice. In the audience, Sydney looked shell-shocked and excited at the same time.

"She's incredible!" Julianna said.

"Isn't she?" Gabby marveled. "She's exactly what this group needs . . . other than me." She laughed and nudged Julianna. "And you! What are you singing?"

Julianna's answer was drowned out by the roar of applause as Viola finished her audition and hurried offstage.

"Gabby Cyprus?" Mr. Wickey announced.

"That's me!" Gabby said, running onto the stage and doing a cartwheel, which got some laughs. After handing in her own sheet music, she busted out Kelly Clarkson's "Catch My Breath." Wow, she had pipes too.

"How do you guys do it?" Julianna asked Viola as she chugged water post-performance. "You didn't even blink out there."

Viola shrugged. "I don't know. I've been listening to my music over and over for days." She pointed to her headphones. "And stages don't scare me, I guess." She smiled. "Want my advice?"

"Yes, please," Julianna said.

"Take a deep breath, and when you get onstage, stare at the back of the auditorium like you have an exit plan. Worked for me."

Julianna's palms were sweating. That stage looked bigger than the one at her old school. Weren't stage sizes regulated? Why was this one so mammoth? She took a deep breath. She could do this. *Shake it off*, she told herself. *Hmm . . . Shake it off! Shake it off! Cause the player's gonna play, play, play . . .*

Great, now she was singing Taylor Swift songs in her head instead of the piece she'd planned on.

"Donna Patel?" Mr. Wickey called.

A small girl with black wavy hair walked onstage and stood there. "Mind if I bring out my sidekick?" she asked in a gravelly voice.

"I'm sorry?" the blond captain said. *"Sidekick?"*

Donna pulled out her right hand, which had a puppet face drawn on it. Some of the guys snickered. "This is Ms. Heel and she'd like to help me sing 'Defying Gravity' from *Wicked*." She didn't wait to be told to start. Julianna was expecting her to sound bad, but Donna's voice was deep with lots of layers. Julianna fidgeted slightly. She couldn't even compete with a puppet. In the audience, Julianna noticed Lidia and Sydney talking heatedly. What was going on? Her phone buzzed and Julianna instinctively looked down. There was a picture of an envelope addressed to her. She enlarged the picture to see who it was from. It was from the Sounds of the Future songwriting contest!

MOM: Look what came!

Julianna wrote back quickly: OPEN IT! Maybe it was a sign that it came that afternoon. Maybe her audition was going to go great. Julianna stared at her phone, waiting for the next picture to come through. When Donna's song was ending, her mom finally sent a picture of the letter.

Dear Julianna Ramirez,

Thank you for your songwriting submission, "Me When There Is No You," to the Sounds of the Future songwriting contest. We were impressed by the thousands of entries we received and the talent that lent their song ideas and voices to our contest. Unfortunately, your song, "Me When There Is No You," was not a winner. We hope you'll consider entering the contest again next year. Keep writing!

–the Sounds of the Future songwriting judges

Her song had lost.

Again.

Julianna breathed heavily and blinked back tears. "Me When There Is No You" was the best song she'd written, but Sounds of the Future wasn't impressed. This was the third songwriting contest she'd entered this year and she'd lost all of them. She pressed delete and erased the picture from existence but not from memory. She was a failure. She obviously couldn't write and she couldn't sing. She wasn't going to make the Nightingales. A single tear fell down her cheek.

MOM: I'm sorry, Ju-Ju. Are you okay?

"Would Ms. Julianna Ramirez take the stage?"

"That's you!" Gabby cheered. She and Viola pushed her toward the stage. "Good luck!"

Between the tears and the darkened stage, Julianna had no clue where she was going. A few smoky, bright-white spotlights were all that was leading the way to the stage. Her pulse was so fast she felt like she had just run four laps around the track.

"Do you have your own music?" the piano player whispered.

Julianna didn't answer her. She closed her eyes for a second to avoid the hot lights and felt like she was back in Miami again. She was at her Tonal Teens audition and Amy, Naya, and the others were cheering her on. Julianna thought she had nailed her audition until Amy called her that night with the bad news.

She didn't belong on this hot, dusty stage and she obviously couldn't write music either. It was time to let her music career fade to black.

"Whenever you're ready, Julianna," Mr. Wickey said.

"Ju-Ju-Julie-ANNA!" she heard one of the boys sing. Someone else started to laugh.

"Isn't that the girl from this morning?" she heard someone say.

"She's the one who fell in the lobby!"

"Sing!" Gabby whispered from the side of the stage.

You didn't make the cut.

Unfortunately, your song was not a winner.

Julianna's mouth tasted like metal. Sweat beaded on her forehead. She was going to bomb this audition too. She clutched her chest. She couldn't breathe.

"Julianna?" Mr. Wickey tried again.

Someone laughed louder.

"I'm sorry. I forgot my sheet music. I'll just run back and get it. Let the next person go instead. Sorry!"

Julianna didn't wait to find out if this was okay with the judges. She just rushed offstage, blowing past Gabby and Viola, and kept going. She had taken one bit of advice from Viola—know where your exits are. She ran toward the glowing red exit sign that signified her freedom.

CHAPTER NINE

Sydney

Sydney could not believe how badly auditions were going. They were only thirty minutes into the process, and other than a few rays of hope, Sydney knew this session was a complete and utter disaster. How could this have happened? She'd had so much hope when she'd walked into the auditorium that afternoon.

Lidia was already there, which had made Sydney breathe a sigh of relief. If Lidia was still mad, she probably wouldn't have shown up. Actually, she would. Lidia was a class act. Either way, Sydney assumed she had gotten through to her: They needed to put the Nightingales first. Mr. Wickey had spotted Sydney walking toward him and smiled.

"Now that everyone is here, I'd love to get started," he'd told them both. "I just want to make one announcement first."

Sydney had taken a seat in the front row and Lidia had sat beside her, which was another good sign.

"As many of you know, I'm the Kingfishers' and Nightingales' club advisor," Mr. Wickey had told the auditorium. "If you are chosen for one of these groups, you'll be making a huge commitment. Both a cappella groups practice a few days a week, compete in various competitions throughout the year, and perform on campus, starting with the Bradley Academy Open House next month." He gave all the captains a stern look. "And while both groups like to have fun with each other, everyone takes their a cappella commitments seriously."

Sydney guessed Mr. Wickey had learned about the anchovy pizzas and the maple syrup flood.

"Sometimes, members are asked to perform outside their groups," Mr. Wickey had added. "I'm pleased to announce that two of our members have been asked to perform at the Naples Center's Fall Music Festival together."

Sydney had sat up straighter in her chair. Being asked to perform at the music festival was a big deal.

"Thanks to their stellar work in the Naples Community Theater production of *In the Heights*, Griffin Mancini and Sydney Marino have been asked to be openers at the Friday night kickoff, which includes a concert by Flo Rida," Mr. Wickey had said.

She and Griffin? People had started clapping and whistling. Sydney had felt like the blood was draining from her face. This couldn't be happening. "No!" she had stood up and shouted. Griffin had looked at her oddly.

So had Mr. Wickey. "I thought you'd be thrilled to be chosen to open up the music festival. Do you have another commitment that weekend?"

Normally, she would have been thrilled. A chance to perform for the public? That was right up her alley! She had looked straight at Lidia to see her reaction. Lidia's face was buried in her notebook. Sydney knew she was probably upset. Here she was telling her how she wanted nothing to do with Griffin, and now the two of them were going to have to spend even more time together practicing for that performance. Alone. A chill went down her spine at the thought. Lidia would be crushed.

"Do you want me to ask if you can be replaced?" Mr. Wickey had said.

Then it was Griffin's turn to have an outburst. "Why? They asked for Sydney."

"I'll do it!" Whitney had volunteered.

Whitney and Griffin? That was not happening either!

"No," Sydney had said quickly. "I mean, I just need to check with my dad first."

Mr. Wickey had smiled. "Okay. If he says you're free, I'll let the festival know. I'll let you two work out the practice details." He had closed his notebook. "On to the auditions."

Sydney was so upset, she had gotten lost in her own thoughts. She didn't hear him talk about how each group would have between ten and twelve members or how there was an emphasis on filling available slots for the group (like sopranos, altos, bass and baritones, and beatboxers). She had tuned out when he had talked about how important stage presence was and had given them an example of the scales they'd each be asked to run. Sydney had even missed Mr. Wickey talking about how each auditioner would need to follow his lead with a series of notes, matching him for tone and harmony. After that, he'd said they'd have three minutes to perform a tune of their choosing, accompanied by the piano player on the stage or set to music on their phones.

All Sydney could think about was herself, Lidia, and Griffin. She knew Lidia was never going to fully forgive her if she had to watch Sydney and Griffin together all the time. Things would be awkward at Nightingales practices too. If there even were Nightingales practices. Sydney had seen the number of girls in the room. The turnout was pitiful. What if there wasn't a beatboxer or two altos to replace the graduating seniors?

"All right, everyone, let's begin." Mr. Wickey had said. People began taking their seats in the auditorium or heading backstage. Lidia and Sydney were already seated side-by-side, not speaking, in the front row next to Dave and Pasqual, who were the Kingfishers' co-captains.

Sydney was an eternal optimist, but her confidence was rattled. All she could think about was the worst-case scenario. What if the Nightingales folded before she and Lidia had a chance to bring them back to their former glory days? What if she and Lidia never made up? What if this was the end of Sydney's singing career? What if, what if, what if?

"Sydney?" Mr. Wickey had asked again. "Are you ready?"

No! Sydney felt hot. All eyes were on her, but she found herself only looking for one person's reaction: Griffin's. As soon as they locked eyes, the strangest thing happened. Suddenly, she felt calm. Things were going to be okay.

But as she sat in the auditorium listening to auditions, she realized that wasn't the case. Where were Julie and her friends? Where was that girl who came to Pinocchio's, who she knew could nail a Beatles tune? Why did Pearl, who hadn't made the cut last year, show up sounding as terrible as ever? Gabby and Viola were good, but Mercedes yelled instead of sang.

A cappella no-no!

Donna, the girl who had showed up at Pinocchio's with a puppet face drawn on her hand, was taking the stage. After giving the puppet a name (Ms. Heel), she dove right into "Defying Gravity." Sydney didn't even have the chance to explain that puppets couldn't be in the Nightingales. And was every girl in here going to do a song from *Wicked*? (It was so refreshing when Viola busted out "Satisfied" from *Hamilton*.) Sydney had to admit Donna's voice was excellent, but the puppet was a deal-breaker. She was about to lean over to Lidia and say just that when Lidia jumped out of her seat and started applauding Donna on her last note.

"That was amazing!" Lidia cheered.

"Um . . ." Sydney slowly stood up. Were they sitting in the same auditorium? "That was really good, but, Donna, we need to see you perform without the use of a puppet."

"Why?" Lidia asked, sounding annoyed.

"Because it's a gimmick," Sydney explained. "The Nightingales aren't about gimmicks."

Lidia folded her arms. "Says who?"

Sydney was nearly at a loss for words. "The a cappella rule book. A cappella groups don't have puppets!"

"The Mouthbreathers in Vero Beach do," Dave reminded her. "They were tough competition last season too."

Lidia motioned to Dave. "Thank you. See?" she said to Sydney. "We *can* have puppets."

What was Lidia doing? They'd talked about doing many things with the Nightingales, but none of them included puppets! Their group was already a laughingstock. They couldn't add a singer with a puppet named Ms. Heel to the mix. They needed to know Donna had stage presence and didn't need a crutch to get up there and perform. "But we don't *want* puppets."

"Maybe you don't, but *I* do," Lidia said gruffly. "You do not get to cast my vote for what I feel and don't feel."

Sydney was taken aback. Was Lidia really going to have a meltdown again in front of everyone? It was bad enough that Mr. Wickey insisted both the boys and girls a cappella groups did tryouts together (he was the club advisor for both, after all), but it was embarrassing fighting in front of the boys. Lidia had promised—*hadn't she?*—that they wouldn't do this here. It was unprofessional. They didn't have enough people auditioning as it was. "I'm not," Sydney said slowly. "What I'm saying is that *we* have always wanted this group to be focused on the singing. *We* never wanted gimmicks and I don't think we should start now." Sydney looked at the stage. "Donna, would you mind trying that again without holding up your, um, fist as Ms. Heel? You have a beautiful voice. We want to hear just you."

Donna clutched her puppet hand close to her chest. "I'm not sure I can sing without her. We're a team."

"That's fine, Donna," Lidia said. "I think we have all we need. You are free to go."

"What? No!" Sydney countered. "I want her to sing again."

"I don't," Lidia said.

"Ladies." Mr. Wickey tried to interrupt.

"Wow, this is better than any Nightingales audition we've seen yet," Dave whispered to Griffin and Pasqual.

"Who cares if she uses a puppet?" Lidia asked. "She's putting herself out there. She's being real! At least she's honest!"

Some of the people auditioning came out of the wings to see what the racket was about.

"What are you talking about?" Sydney asked.

Lidia's whole body was shaking. "I just mean . . . I . . . she's not acting like other people I know!"

Sydney put her hands on her hips and tried not to look as mortified as she felt. Why was Lidia airing their dirty laundry again? She caught a glimpse of Griffin's face. It was grim while Dave and Pasqual were still laughing. "Are you referring to me?"

"Yes! It's always all about you, you, you! 'Don't be upset, Lidia. Think of the Nightingales and competitions!'" Lidia mimicked. "God forbid you stop for a second and think about your best friend's feelings." She paused for a second, then shouted, "Your apology was so fake!"

Sydney's jaw dropped. "It was not!"

Griffin cleared his throat. "Uh, guys, do you really want to do this here?" he asked.

Lidia and Sydney both looked at him. "Yes!"

Lidia's voice was shaky. "You gave the classic 'Sydney apology,' which is to gloss over the actual apology." Her face was red. "You really hurt me, Syd, and you don't even care. And now I don't either." She looked around, suddenly realizing they had an audience. "I'm sorry," she said to Mr. Wickey. "I forgot there is somewhere I have to be."

Sydney was fuming. "Lidia! We're in the middle of auditions!" Lidia kept walking. "Fine! Leave! You're good at yelling then storming out of places! Go!" Lidia whirled around, tears in her eyes. Okay, maybe that was taking things too far. "Wait. Lidia! Wait!"

Whitney appeared by Sydney's side. "Wow, some captain she is."

"Are you really going to let her walk out in the middle of auditions?" Micayla asked. "Maybe you should go after her."

Sydney's chest was rising and falling rapidly. Her cheeks burned. Lidia had made a fool of her again! "No," Sydney said stiffly. She smoothed her hair and sat back down, tapping a pen on her notebook. "My job is to stay right here. I'm sorry," she told the others, looking longer at Mr. Wickey and avoiding Griffin's gaze. "Let's start again, please."

Mr. Wickey ran a hand through his hair. "Okay. Ladies and gentlemen, I apologize for the interruption. We're going to proceed with auditions without Ms. Sato."

Sydney was too busy staring at the white space on her loose-leaf paper to witness Whitney and Micayla high-five with glee.

CHAPTER TEN

Julianna

Julianna gripped her knees, hung her head, and took deep, gulping breaths, rocking back and forth on the ground outside the theater's back door.

It was over. She wasn't near the stage anymore. *It's going to be okay*, she told herself. She was thankful Gabby and Viola didn't follow her. When she finally felt her breathing slow, she stood up and leaned against the theater wall.

Her first day at Bradley had been an epic fail. How was she going to face her new classmates after running out on them *twice*? And what music extracurricular option was she left with now? She banged her head on the wall she was leaning against. Chorus, that's what.

Julianna clutched the small silver musical note she wore around her neck. It was a gift from her mom for her birthday. It was meant to be a reminder that all roads in Julianna's life led to music. But so far, every road she went down was a dead end. How many more times could she put herself out there and fail?

Julianna didn't know how much time had passed when her phone buzzing got her attention. She looked at the group text.

NAYA: I'm with Amy! We're thinking of you. How was your first day?

Julianna took another deep breath, feeling the warm air fill her lungs. She might as well be honest. These were her closest friends.

JULIANNA: Terrible.

NAYA: Why???

JULIANNA: I chickened out of trying out for the school's a cappella group.

NAYA: Aww! Who cares? Try out for volleyball instead. You're good!

JULIANNA: Thanks, but every student needs a music program here. Lucky me.

Julianna was too embarrassed to tell her friends she'd lost another songwriting contest too, so she left that part out.

NAYA: Eek. That is a problem. You'll figure it out. We love you, Ju-Ju!

AMY: Join the chorus! You can stand in the back and sway! LOL!

Ouch! She knew Amy was kidding, but didn't she realize not making the Tonal Teens was a sore point for her?

JULIANNA: ☹

NAYA: She's kidding!

AMY: JK! Their loss! How's the songwriting going? Got anything TT could use this competition season?

Julianna sighed. It was just like Amy to change the subject. Julianna had given her a song for the Tonal Teens to use last season and it had won them gold. Amy was forever trying to get Julianna to write for the group, but Julianna was hesitant. It still hurt too much. Besides, she had been saving her music for the songwriting contests, which required original, unperformed songs. The fact that Julianna had music she wouldn't give to the Tonal Teens seemed to drive Amy nuts.

JULIANNA: Nothing yet! Maybe today's screwup will give me inspiration. ☺

NAYA: That's our girl! Don't let an audition beat you. And you're too good for general chorus. Get back in there and try out! What do you have to lose?

What do you have to lose? Naya had a point. If she didn't go in there and audition, then she was definitely going to be stuck with general chorus or worse—having to learn the tuba. At least with the Tonal Teens she had tried. Would she kick herself if she didn't audition? The crowds had probably thinned out by now. Maybe no one other than Gabby and Viola knew she was missing. After all, she did say she was running back to get her sheet music. Julianna smiled. This might work!

She stood up and banged on the theater door, hoping Gabby and Viola or someone else would hear her. It felt like she was banging forever before a custodian finally opened the door and Julianna rushed in past him.

"If you're here to audition for the a cappella groups, they're over," he said.

Julianna stopped short. "They're done already? How?" She hadn't been last on the list. Had they finished early?

The custodian shook his head. "Not sure. There was a lot of yelling. Crazy a cappella kids. Left a ton of papers behind. No one cleans up after themselves anymore." He grabbed his broom and walked away.

Julianna went to the stage to be sure. The custodian was right. It was a ghost town. The auditorium lights were dim and everyone was gone. The only thing left behind was a stack of sheet music on the piano. She walked over and picked up the piano music. It seemed like everyone had either sung a song from *Wicked* or *Hamilton*.

She'd screwed up. A future in a cappella was not in the cards. She sank down on the piano bench.

"If you want to stay and use the piano, I don't mind," the custodian said. "I like music to work to."

Julianna glanced at her phone. Her mother wouldn't be picking her up for another half hour anyway. She didn't want to run into anyone on campus. She was upset and tired and when she felt like that, music was the cure.

"Thanks." She opened the piano key lid, flipping through the *Wicked* songbook till she found what she was looking for. "What Is This Feeling?" was her favorite tune in the show. She loved how Elphaba and Glinda started out the musical as enemies and eventually found a harmony that worked for the two of them.

"What is this feeling so sudden and new?" Julianna sang, doing the Glinda part, which was always harder for her as an alto. She could barely hit Glinda's high notes, but she gave it her best shot as the song flipped back and forth between the two singers. It felt good to sing. As she hit the first stanza, her voice reached a crescendo and her fingers moved over the piano keys more feverishly. She was so into the song, she didn't notice a girl had jumped up onstage until she was standing directly over the piano. Julianna froze. It was Sydney Marino.

"Keep playing!" Sydney whispered, smiling encouragingly. *"Let's just say, I loathe it all!"* she sang in a rich, high voice. She was a soprano, and a really good one. She motioned for Julianna to keep playing. *"Every little trait, however small . . . ,"* she continued to sing, and without thinking, Julianna joined in.

It took a few lines for it to happen, but their voices began to harmonize. Maybe that's why the song felt so electric. When Julianna ran a line, Sydney was right there with the next one. They were sparring in song, and it worked. Julianna hadn't sung in front of anyone but her mother in a while, but this felt right. Suddenly, she didn't want the song to end.

"And I will be loathing you my whole life long!" the two girls sang, holding the last note until Julianna's fingers finally left the ivory keys.

The custodian broke out into applause. "That was amazing!" he said, clapping harder. "You two have my vote!"

Sydney jumped up and down too. *"You* were amazing! That was the best audition I've heard in forever!"

"Really?" Julianna said in surprise. "But that wasn't an audition. I was looking for my sheet music and I guess I lost track of time and didn't realize you guys finished up." *I chickened out.*

"But you were going to audition so this counts," Sydney said matter-of-factly. "I've been sitting in the back of the auditorium in the dark, sulking over the fact that we don't have enough talent for the Nightingales to pull from. And then I heard you start to sing. You're just what the group needs—what *I* need after today—a true talent. I say that was an audition, and if it was an audition, I'm officially telling you, you're in!"

Julianna felt like she had stopped breathing. Was she dreaming? This couldn't be real. When she put herself out there, she fell flat on her face. That's how her life worked. But now she was being thrown a musical lifeline. "You can do that without asking anyone?"

Sydney's face darkened. "Yes, because I am the only captain who cares today."

Julianna wasn't sure what that meant, but she nodded.

Sydney held out her hand and grinned. "Who are you, by the way?"

"Julianna Ramirez."

Sydney pumped Julianna's hand. "Nice to meet you, Julianna. Welcome to the Nightingales."

CHAPTER ELEVEN

Lidia

Lidia knew how she must look to the people on the bus—like she had lost her mind. On the ride from Bradley to the Naples downtown area, she had spent the whole time mumbling to herself about puppeteers, a cappella, and the Nightingales. Sydney had made her so mad!

"This is not an off-Broadway production of *Dear Evan Hansen*," she said aloud to herself as she walked down Naples's Fifth Avenue, passing boutique art galleries and jewelry stores that sold dolphin earrings and starfish decorated on pretty much everything. "It's a high school a cappella group! Why knock talent even if it does come with a puppet?" She flung open the door to Kyle's Candy Shoppe. "Were we that good when we auditioned freshman year? No. Sydney was really pitchy, so there!"

Ahh . . . The smell of chocolate mixed with taffy and fudge instantly calmed her down. Kyle's shop, while much smaller, reminded her of *Charlie and the Chocolate Factory* (which was still one of her favorite books). Some days she stood and stared wistfully at the twelve-dollar salted-caramel-covered giant pretzels that were out of her budget for an after-school snack. Other days, she just grabbed a water like most of the dancers from her studio did before class. But most days she broke down and bought an eighth of a pound of chocolate wafer nonpareils covered in sprinkles. She'd eat them slowly on her way to class. Today, Lidia knew she needed at least half a pound of chocolate to get through the afternoon!

Kids in the shop lingered around a giant chocolate fountain where you could dip pretzels and fruit for a dollar apiece. Lidia closed her eyes and savored the smell of caramel before walking to the counter where Kyle was helping a lone customer.

"Hey, Lidia! How was your first day of school?"

"It played out like a scene from a horror movie," she said, pulling her wallet out of her bag. "The only way I'll make it through my dance class is with some chocolate. Can I get a half pound of nonpareils?"

Kyle's smile faded. "Actually, someone just beat you to the last ones. We won't have more till tomorrow."

"WHAT?" Lidia flung herself against the glass candy counter. A mother walking nearby looked startled. "Who stole my chocolate?" Kyle's eyes shifted to the right. Lidia's jaw dropped and she became momentarily flustered. It was Jack from the bus and he was holding a clear bag of nonpareils. *Her* nonpareils! "You? What are you doing here?"

"I could ask you the same question," said Jack, his mouth curving into a half-smile as he reached into the bag of chocolate and took one sprinkled-color wafer out and popped it into his mouth. He had a great smile, which made her feel flustered. "This is my favorite candy shop. Reminds me of *Charlie and the Chocolate Factory*."

This was uncanny. "Me too." Lidia pointed to his bag. "And those are my favorite chocolates."

"Same. I buy them every week."

"So do I," she said, "until today."

"Do you two know each other?" Kyle leaned over the counter. "You guys keep my nonpareil business afloat. You both buy them every week."

Lidia narrowed her eyes at Jack. "You're the one who is always buying the nonpareils? Last week I had to buy peanut butter clusters because Kyle ran out. And now you did it again."

Jack ran a hand through his messy black hair. "Sorry, but it's not my fault you only buy an eighth of a pound."

"How do you know I only buy an eighth of a pound?" Lidia looked at Kyle accusingly.

Kyle looked guilty. "I always beg Jack to leave an eighth of a pound for you, but sometimes he persuades me to give him all the chocolate I've got." He looked at Jack. "He can be quite persuasive."

Jack's dark eyes gleamed from behind his glasses. "I've been told I'm quite the charmer."

Lidia thought back to how Jack knew their bus driver's name and people on the route personally. "More like thief," she teased.

Jack held out his hand and grinned. "Nice to officially meet you, Ms. Nonpareils. I'm Jack Nielson."

Lidia shook his hand. "Lidia Sato, and I'll decide if it's nice to meet you after you tell me whether I can buy back those nonpareils." She looked at Kyle. "I need a half pound or more today."

Kyle made a face. "Whoa, it really was a horror-movie kind of day, huh?"

Jack eyed her curiously as he swung the bag of chocolate in his hand. "I was looking forward to this chocolate fix after my day too. How do I know you need it more than I do?"

"Ooh!" Kyle clapped his hands. "It's a chocolate battle. Who needs the sweet stuff more?"

Jack's eyes lit up. "I'm game, Lidia. Are you?"

Lidia was in no mood for games, but she needed those nonpareils. They were going to be the highlight of her day. "Fine. But you go first." She wasn't spilling her guts to him if he didn't do the same.

Jack made his already messy hair stand up even more. "Okay, so my laptop, Mr. Krinkle—"

Lidia burst out laughing. "Your laptop has a name?"

"Yes." Jack looked hurt. "Doesn't everyone's?"

Lidia shook her head. "Nope."

"Well, mine does, or did. Mr. Krinkle, who has been with me since middle school, by the way, blew up this morning, taking all the backup for the app I'm creating with it." Jack started talking really fast. "While all that info should be in the cloud, it turns out my cloud hasn't been backing up all summer, so it's lost. The app contest deadline is in a month, which means I am now going to lose and will never have enough money to open my own nonpareil factory." He hung his head and tried to look sad.

"Tragic," Kyle agreed.

"RIP, Mr. Krinkle," Lidia said, trying not to smile. "Still, you haven't heard my story yet. How would you feel if you found out your best friend kissed the boy you'd liked since middle school and hid it from you? And then you had to suffer through a cappella auditions with the two of them, who are also now singing a duet together at the Naples Music Festival?"

"Whoa," Kyle and Jack said at the same time.

Lidia couldn't stop now. "The worst part? When she asked to talk to me before auditions, I thought it was to apologize. But no! She just wanted to make sure I wouldn't make her look bad at the auditions."

Jack held out the chocolates. "You win. Take the whole pound. I don't need it, even if my cat did die last week."

Lidia looked horrified. "Your cat died?"

Jack's face broke into another grin. He really did have the best smile she'd ever seen. For a moment, she even thought she felt a flutter in her chest.

"Nah," Jack said. "I don't even have a cat, but if I did, that and Mr. Krinkle might have beaten your heartbreak story."

Lidia took the chocolate and held it to her chest. "Thanks. How much do I owe you?"

Jack waved her off. "My gift to you. I'd need a truckload of chocolate if my best friend did that to me. And if you don't mind me saying so, that guy is a fool for picking your friend over you."

Lidia blushed. "You don't even know my friend."

"Doesn't matter," Jack said. "I just know. He picked wrong."

Lidia's face heated up even more. "Thanks." She opened the bag of chocolate and poured some pieces into her hand. She offered them to Jack. He popped a nonpareil into his mouth.

"Aah . . . chocolate makes everything better," he said.

They stared at each other goofily. That's when Lidia remembered. She had somewhere she needed to be—dance class!

"I have to go." She hesitated a moment. Would she run into him again? "Thanks again for the chocolate." How many times was she going to say thank you? She sounded ridiculous.

Jack checked the time. "I'll walk out with you. I have to be somewhere too."

Kyle handed Jack a giant peanut butter cup. "For being a good sport." He looked at Lidia. "See you tomorrow?"

"Maybe."

"You too, Jack?" Kyle asked. If Lidia didn't know any better, she'd think Kyle was trying to set them up.

"Definitely!" Jack high-fived him, then stepped out the door behind Lidia. They danced around each other till they realized they were going in the same direction. "My computer coding class is down the block," he explained.

"Pixels?" Lidia asked. "That's next door to Integral Dance Arts. That's where I'm headed."

"I guess we're walking together then." Jack put his hand on his heart. "I promise not to steal any chocolate."

"I was hoping you would, otherwise I'll eat it all myself." She held out the open bag.

As Jack took another handful, Lidia studied his face. She liked how his freckles bridged his nose.

"Nice dance bag, by the way," he said. "That's how I banged into you on the bus in the first place. I was staring at Sailor Moon."

Lidia glanced at her dance bag, which had a small Sailor Moon emblem on it. Sailor Moon was still her favorite anime cartoon. When she was younger, she dressed as Sailor Moon for Halloween five years in a row. "You're a fan?"

"Fan?" Jack said in surprise. "I don't cosplay Tuxedo Mask for nothing. I've got quite the top hat."

Lidia's eyebrows arched. He knew who Tuxedo Mask was? He fought alongside Sailor Moon. "You're into cosplay? I've always wanted to try it, but my best friend said dressing up as a character when it wasn't Halloween was weird."

Jack raised his right eyebrow. "I'm really not liking this so-called best friend of yours."

"Sydney's actually pretty fun," Lidia said instinctively. "You know, when she isn't kissing boys I like."

"I'll take your word for it." Jack kept up as they turned the corner. "There's a cosplay convention in Naples coming up that my friends and I are going to." They stopped in front of Pixels. "It's kind of nerdy, but not nerdy." Lidia laughed. "It's the usual stuff—costume contests, meet and greets, and comic book panel discussions. Any chance you want to come?"

He wanted to see her again? And in costume? There was that fluttery feeling in her chest again. "I'll think about it."

Jack opened the door to the computer lab. "I'll convince you next time I see you on the bus or at Kyle's."

He was going to look for her. Her face suddenly felt warm. "Then I guess I'll be seeing you."

"Have a good class, Ms. Nonpareil."

"You too," Lidia said, walking away. As she did, her phone pinged. Her mother had sent her three texts.

MOM: How was the audition? Good talent pool?

MOM: Did enough people try out? I told a new student, Julianna, to come today.

MOM: I'm sure it went great! With you and Sydney as captains, this is the year the Nightingales make a comeback! You'll be at competitions in no time. Judges are going to love you guys. It will look great on college apps next year too.

Lidia's mom had a bad habit of sending paragraphs as text messages. How was she going to explain to her mom that she had walked out of auditions? Her mom loved telling people how Lidia was part of a living Nightingales legacy and how she had started the group and Lidia was going to save it. But Lidia wasn't sure that could be done anymore. Thanks to her outbursts, the Nightingales' reputation was more in the dumps than ever. They'd be lucky if they even got a team together. If they didn't have enough girls, there wouldn't even be a team anymore. Hmm . . . that would mean she wouldn't have to see Sydney and Griffin together.

Lidia's stomach lurched. That was a terrible thing to think!

Lidia arrived at the dance studio and walked in to the sounds of ballet music competing with a hip-hop song in another classroom. The lobby was a flurry of activity with girls coming and going and parents paying for classes or talking about costumes with the receptionist. Lidia flattened herself against the wall to stay out of the way. She didn't mind all the chaos around her. She loved watching people lace up their pointe shoes or tap down the long hallways, which were filled with black-and-white pictures of the senior competition team. When the room cleared out, Lidia stepped up to the front desk.

"Hi, Lidia," the receptionist said. "Doesn't Pattie Ann have an appointment with you tomorrow?"

"Yes," said Lidia, feeling unsure now. "But I wound up having some free time today so I thought I'd see if she had some time to talk."

The receptionist smiled. "I'm sure she does. She's not tracking for another fifteen minutes. Head on back to the studio."

Lidia wondered what Miss Pattie Ann wanted to talk to her about. She hoped it wasn't to say she hadn't signed up for enough classes. It killed her to think about how she wouldn't be at the studio every day like she had been for the past ten weeks. She'd agonized over what class to take when she could only do one—barre work or hip-hop? Pointe or jazz? Tap or modern? She still wasn't sure signing up for pointe was the right way to go.

The music grew louder as she reached the back studio. Miss Pattie Ann was practicing choreography in front of the mirrors. Lidia stood there and watched her teacher glide across the room. She didn't acknowledge Lidia till the song ended.

"What do you think?" Miss Pattie Ann asked, sounding slightly out of breath. "Think the class will be able to master that combination?"

"We'll give it our best shot," Lidia said. "I know we were going to talk tomorrow, but I wound up having some extra time today."

Miss Pattie Ann grinned. "Wonderful." She threw her right leg up on the barre and stretched. "I've been really impressed by your footwork this summer. You've managed to keep up with the competition girls and hold your own with some of our seniors. That's not such an easy thing to do."

"Thanks." Lidia blushed. "I really liked the classes." "Liked" wasn't the word for it. Dancing had made her summer. She loved how it felt to master a tricky routine or go across the floor practicing leaps and turns. She got goose bumps when she watched her class perform numbers in the mirror. She found herself doing choreography to songs in her head all the time now.

"What would you say to auditioning for the senior competition team?" Miss Pattie Ann asked her as she stretched her arms into a graceful arch over the barre.

"Audition?" Lidia's heart stopped. "I thought you had to be a junior to try out for the team."

"Normally, yes, but we had more seniors on last year's team than usual, so more slots have opened up." She looked at Lidia. "I think you could fill one of them, if you're interested."

It took all her willpower not to scream "YES!" "How do I try out?"

"You'd come in during tryouts this weekend and learn a routine with others auditioning. Then you'd each get a chance to perform in front of me and some of the other teachers next week. We'll be announcing new team members the following week. It would all happen quickly."

"I'd love to be considered," Lidia said. It would be too much to throw her arms around Miss Pattie Ann and squeal, but that's what she wanted to do.

"Wonderful!" Miss Pattie Ann grinned. "I know this is a bit premature, but if you make the team, you'll dive into practices. Usually, competition classes are five days a week, several classes a day. Getting ready for competition season takes a lot of work. Think you could handle that?"

Lidia's heart sank. How would she fit in all those classes with Nightingales practices too? There was no way she could pull off both. She'd have to choose: Nightingales or dance, and she'd already committed to the Nightingales. If she left them flat, and they had enough girls for a team, her captain spot would need to be replaced. Lidia could just see Whitney and Micayla trying to oust Sydney so they could step in. Lidia could also imagine her own family's reaction. Grandma Evie was so proud of Lidia being a Nightingale like Lidia's mom had been before her. What would they say when she told them she'd given it up? Her heart started to thump in time with the music in another room. There was no logical way to make this all work, and yet Lidia could not handle turning down the opportunity.

Her head was stubbornly telling her not to. In fact, it was singing lines from *Hamilton*.

I'm not throwing away my shot!

Alexander Hamilton had the right idea. She'd figure out the logistics *if* and when she actually made the team.

Lidia pointed and flexed her foot inside her street shoes. "I *know* I can handle it."

She hoped she was right.

CHAPTER TWELVE

Sydney

The Nightingales team—or lack of—hadn't even been decided yet, but somehow Sydney already had practice with Griffin for the Naples Music Festival.

Standing outside one of the Bradley music rooms that students could reserve for individual practices, Sydney stalled. She could hear Griffin playing the piano, but couldn't get herself to open the door. She'd put her hand on the knob, then turn and walk away. Attempt to open the door, then run down the hall. They only had the room for a half hour and she'd already wasted ten minutes. Maybe that was a good thing. She wasn't sure she could handle all that alone time with Griffin. Her head knew this was a bad idea, but her heart kept singing, *I kissed Griffin Mancini and I liked it.*

One week ago, Lidia had threatened the existence of the Nightingales with her very public—and embarrassing—outburst. Since then, they still hadn't spoken or gotten together to see if they had enough girls to put together a team. Meanwhile, the Kingfishers team had been announced and they'd already started practicing. Sydney's a cappella career was in the toilet.

Sydney placed her hand on the doorknob again. She felt herself get yanked forward along with the door.

"Oh, it's you." Dave, the Kingfishers' co-captain, looked less than thrilled to see Sydney in the now-open doorway. "You owe me one hundred and fifty dollars for the pizzas you ruined plus money for an allergy shot."

"Dave," Griffin warned. He was seated at the piano.

"Well, she does! She knows what she did," Dave grumbled.

Sydney gave her best innocent expression. "I don't know what you're talking about. Why do I owe you money? Are you doing a fund-raiser?"

"Oh, you know," Dave said, his frown deepening so much it gave him wrinkles. "Delivering a sunflower bouquet to our first practice? Everyone knows sunflowers make me sneeze for hours. And don't get me started on the pizzas. You ruined eight pies!"

Sydney side-eyed Griffin. "Still no clue what you're talking about."

Dave mumbled something under his breath and stormed off. Sydney knew she would pay for the flowers and pizza pranks, but at the moment she wasn't even sure she had a team. How could the Kingfishers really get her back?

"Ready to make music together?" Griffin asked.

Sydney's heart was going to need paddles to survive this practice.

She turned back to the door. "I just came by to tell you that I have to go home and study or I'm going to tank tomorrow's math test."

Griffin hit a wrong note on the piano. He looked too cute to stare at for too long. He'd removed his blazer and tie and his button-down blue shirt was open to reveal a beachy graphic tee underneath. "Don't you have a meeting with Mr. Wickey after this?"

"Yes!" Sydney realized, turning away again. "I really should be waiting outside his door."

"You have time. He's at a faculty meeting." Griffin started playing again. "He won't be back for a while, so you might as well practice with me first." Sydney opened her mouth to protest. "Or we could study for your math test. In addition to being the best singer at this school—" She cleared her throat. "*Tied* for being the best singer at this school," he corrected, "I am a math god. We can practice for the festival *and* I'll help you study before Mr. Wickey returns." He slid over on the piano bench. "What do you have to lose?"

Lidia? Sydney thought.

The melody Griffin was playing was pretty. "Come on. If you're nice, I'll even share my peanut-butter-and-Nutella sandwich with you."

Griffin had made her one over the summer at play practice. No one could understand how they'd both liked the combo. They agreed it was like eating a peanut butter cup on bread.

"Or we could go out to eat sometime." He looked at her seriously. "I think we'd have fun."

She knew they would. They had more in common than she could have imagined. But she couldn't do that to Lidia. She was going to burst into flames for wanting a boy she knew she couldn't have. Sydney didn't know what to do. She was so tempted—to sing with him, sit on the piano bench next to him, and go out to dinner with him.

Griffin stopped playing. "Does you acting funny have anything to do with Lidia?"

Sydney felt her heart stop. "What?"

"I heard some things about you and me and Lidia," he said awkwardly. His cheeks were turning pink. "I didn't know she . . . I hope you guys are okay, is all I'm saying."

"I think she is," Sydney said, her cheeks growing warm too. "Anyway, what happened isn't your fault, it's mine."

"What do you mean?" Griffin asked.

"Never mind," Sydney said quickly. She didn't want to get into this with him.

"Maybe we should start singing. Why don't we warm up with one of your favorite tunes?" Griffin started to play again. Sydney recognized the song right away. She sat down next to him. Wordlessly, he handed her the song music. He was playing "Seasons of Love" from *Rent*. As Griffin played, Sydney let herself get lost in the music. On cue, he started to sing.

"Five hundred twenty-five thousand six hundred minutes."

Even as Griffin played, his eyes never left Sydney's face. It was the first time they had sung this song together and yet Sydney could feel the music in every inch of her body. When a song felt right, it felt right. Sydney couldn't imagine singing this with anyone other than him. They had great harmony, and Sydney had a feeling it wasn't just in song.

"Seasons of love," they both sang, smiling.

As Griffin played the last notes, their faces inched closer. They held the last note as long as possible. The music stopped, but neither of them moved. *He's going to kiss me again*, she thought. This time, she wanted him to. *Badly*. But she knew it was wrong so she turned away.

"Griffin, I . . ."

The door to the room opened and Lidia stuck her head in. When she saw the two of them together, her face fell.

Sydney was in major treble. Trouble!

Well, technically it was treble trouble.

"Oh. I—sorry!" Lidia shut the door.

Sydney jumped up, her heart pumping wildly. She'd done nothing wrong this time, but she'd thought about it. "I should go."

Griffin seemed to get it. "I know."

"Sorry," Sydney said and Griffin nodded. "Rain check?"

In more ways than one?

Sydney rushed down the hall after Lidia. What was going on between them wasn't right. She was a fixer. She had to fix things. "Sorry about that," she said, rushing to walk next to her. "We were just practicing for the music festival."

"Good for you." Lidia looked straight ahead, her ponytail swishing wildly as she headed to Mr. Wickey's office.

Weird. Lidia only wore her hair in a ponytail on dance class days, but Sydney could have sworn Lidia had said she was going to take class on Mondays. Today was Thursday.

"Were you looking for me?" Sydney asked hopefully. "We should probably talk about auditions before we meet with Mr. Wickey, right?"

Lidia hesitated. "Yes. No. I don't know." She threw her hands up. "If *you* wanted to talk, why didn't you come looking for me before now?"

"I thought you needed space." Sydney gaped. "Was I wrong?"

Lidia narrowed her eyes. "No, but shouldn't you be trying to make things right?"

"I am! I mean, I want to, but you've been so mad I don't know how to act," Sydney admitted. "I also thought my best friend would have talked to me in private instead of airing what's going on between us to the entire a cappella community."

"What choice did you give me?" Lidia complained.

"I know." Sydney stared at her glittery Tom's slip-ons (a girl with a uniform had to add bling where she could). They were yelling at each other again.

The last time Lidia had been this upset with her was the Snow Ball in eighth grade. Sydney had found a pale-blue dress with a sparkly silver hem online and knew it was the one. The price tag said otherwise, and she refused to ask her dad to drop that kind of money on a dress she'd only wear once. She stuck it in her online shopping cart anyway and forgot about it. Then her mom had ordered it without Syd even asking. Her mom rarely did stuff like that, so the dress took on a whole new level of meaning.

When Lidia had shown Sydney the exact same dress hanging in her closet and said she was planning on wearing it to the dance, the two had fought. Sydney talked about it meaning so much because it came from her mom, and Lidia went on and on about how this was her chance to get noticed by Griffin. They had both stormed off without deciding who was going to wear the dress.

Two days later, Lidia had texted: The dress was meant to be worn by you. It told me so. Blue is more your color anyway.

That was Lidia. Always the bigger person. And what did she get in return? A best friend who kissed the love of her life. *Oh, Lidia . . . I am the worst*, Sydney thought. "I hate fighting with you," Sydney whispered.

Lidia sighed. "I hate fighting with you too." Sydney looked up hopefully. "But I don't know how to get past what you did. Even if it wasn't your fault, you let it happen and then you hid it from me. How did you think I'd react?"

"I'm so sor—" Sydney started to apologize when Mr. Wickey's door opened.

"Oh good, you're both here!" Mr. Wickey said. "Do you want to come in?"

Her chance to get through to Lidia was gone. Reluctantly, she grabbed her things and followed Lidia into the office. His room was basically an oversized closet with just enough space for a desk, a guitar, and a bookcase overflowing with songbooks and pictures of him and his wife.

Sydney looked straight at the photographs to avoid eye contact with Lidia. She was afraid if she looked at her, she'd burst into tears. She placed one hand on her crossed knee to keep her legs from bouncing. Her mind kept trying to reboot, but all she could think about was their fight. She and Lidia had never argued like this before.

Mr. Wickey squeezed himself behind his messy desk and took a seat. "I wanted to talk to you two about auditions. I was pretty disappointed in how things went."

Both girls looked down.

"When you two were named co-captains, I was sure the Nightingales were going to make a comeback, but you two haven't even gotten together to pick a team."

"I'm sorry," Lidia said, surprising Sydney. "I shouldn't have walked out and left you and Sydney to handle the auditions. It wasn't fair to the group."

"But in the end, it worked out," Sydney offered, hoping it helped. "We finished auditions and I found a great alto for the group. Julianna Ramirez." It was Lidia's turn to look intrigued.

Mr. Wickey nodded. "Julianna sang for me this week and I agree she'd be a great addition to the group." He slid the audition sign-up sheet over to the girls. "You don't have a huge pool to pick from. I'm told a lot of girls were turned off by the fighting the two of you have been doing." Both girls starting talking at once. "But I'm hopeful you can put that all aside for the sake of the group you wanted to run."

"Yes," Lidia and Sydney agreed quietly.

"The Kingfishers have already made, and notified, all of their picks and held their first practice," he added, "so I was hoping you two could pick your team members this afternoon so you can move forward. Headmistress Sato is anxious to see the Nightingales practicing. She's a huge fan, as you know." Mr. Wickey tried unsuccessfully not to smirk.

"Oh, I know," Lidia said.

Mr. Wickey gave them a look. "Although I heard not much got done at the boys' first practice because they had so many distractions."

Sydney didn't even blink an eye.

Mr. Wickey leaned over his notes. "Anyway, the Nightingales need to start practicing too if they want to be ready for the Turn It Up competition in November. Have you two discussed your choices yet?"

"No," both girls said.

"You need ten to twelve girls to compete in the competitions we chose for the year and you have . . . fifteen girls to pick from."

Both girls looked over the sign-up sheet. Sydney and Lidia were two picks, which meant they needed at least eight of the fifteen girls they'd seen. Micayla and Whitney, as much as Sydney couldn't stand them, were musts, as were Gabby and Viola, who were good as well. Julianna was a shoo-in, but that still meant they needed at least three girls. And Sydney didn't like any of her choices.

"Sydney?" Mr. Wickey asked. "What are you thinking?"

"Whitney, Micayla, Gabby, and Viola for sure," she said.

"Lidia?" Mr. Wickey asked.

"I agree," she said.

Whew!

"And I'd like to nominate Julianna because she's unbelievably talented," Sydney said.

"I didn't hear her sing," Lidia pointed out.

"I'm vouching for her, and Mr. Wickey heard her too," Sydney said. "That should be enough."

Lidia's face changed. "Well, it's not enough. I have to hear her too. Or you need to give me Donna."

"Puppet Girl?" Sydney scoffed. "Never."

"Then no Julianna." Lidia sounded snippy, which wasn't her style. Lidia usually trusted Sydney's judgment.

"Julianna is talented," Sydney pointed out.

"So is Donna," Lidia insisted.

Mr. Wickey's chair squeaked. Both girls looked at him. "Ladies, this is ridiculous. Why can't you have both girls? You still need four slots filled."

"One should go to Mercedes too," Lidia said. "She's loud, but that can be worked on."

"She just yells," Sydney disagreed.

"Do you have a better idea?" Lidia asked. "Do you want the girl who did the 'Cups' song?"

"No." Sydney sank lower in her chair.

"Then we don't have enough girls," Lidia snapped.

"Whose fault is that?" Sydney countered. "You scared them all away."

"That's your fault! If you hadn't done what you did to me, I wouldn't have been mad."

"You have a right to be mad, but you don't have a right to ruin the Nightingales because of it! It's like you're trying to sabotage the group!"

The room was silent.

Maybe Sydney had gone too far.

Mr. Wickey cleared his throat. "When you two lobbied *me* last spring to become the youngest co-captains of this team, I remember thinking, 'They're too young. We should go with Micayla and

Whitney, who will be a year older.' But you two convinced me." He laughed. "You had a clear vision for the Nightingales that was so impressive I couldn't say no. You continued to prove yourselves all summer with emails and song arrangements."

Sydney beamed. That was all her.

"Now it's the second week of school and you two are arguing at auditions, accusing each other of sabotaging the group, and disagreeing on team picks." Mr. Wickey cocked his head. "This does not sound like the girls I chose to be captains."

Sydney watched Lidia scratch her right eyebrow. Whenever Lidia was stressed, she adopted this quirky habit. "We're sorry," Sydney said. "Things have changed since the summer. It's . . . complicated."

How had things between her and Lidia gotten this bad? Best friends fought sometimes, but they made up eventually. Maybe Lidia didn't want to forgive her right now, but she couldn't stay mad at her forever.

"This is my fault," Sydney blurted out. "I wasn't fair to Lidia and I apologized, but she has a right to still be upset." She smiled encouragingly at Lidia. "Last week was a hiccup, but we take our co-captain status seriously and we're looking forward to leading this team to their first a cappella victory in five years. No matter what's gone on between us, we are committed to working together as a team."

"No," Lidia said quietly.

"No?" Sydney did a double take. "To what part?"

Lidia looked at Mr. Wickey. "I don't think the two of us can work together as co-captains. I'm sorry I wasted your time."

"What?" Sydney freaked out. Lidia wouldn't look at her. "You can't quit."

"Lidia, are you sure about this?" Mr. Wickey asked.

Lidia's voice broke. "I'm sure."

"Don't do this," Sydney begged. "We can work together, I'm sure of it."

"We can't even agree on a team," Lidia said. "How are we going to run one together? I think it's best if I step down."

"Your mom will kill you," Sydney blurted out. "And you have to take a music extracurricular anyway. What are you going to take instead?"

Lidia's eyes narrowed. "I'll worry about my mom, thanks. And what activity I take is not your business." She looked at Mr. Wickey. "I would like to resign."

"If you're sure," Mr. Wickey said. Lidia nodded.

Sydney couldn't believe what she was hearing. "But if Lidia resigns, that means we need five more members!"

"And a new co-captain, or co-captains," Mr. Wickey said awkwardly. "The a cappella teams always have two leaders for this very reason."

Sydney's heart broke. Whitney and Micayla would do their best to oust her and take the roles themselves. It's what they'd always wanted. Lidia had to know this. "Lidia, please," she begged. "Don't do this."

Lidia shook her head. "I'm sorry. I should go." She grabbed her bag and went to the door.

"I appreciate you being honest with us, Lidia," Mr. Wickey said.

119

"Good luck with your extracurricular this year." Lidia nodded, briefly glanced at Sydney, and ducked out.

"I'll be right back," Sydney told Mr. Wickey. She caught up with Lidia down the hall. "I said I was sorry! What more do you want me from me?"

Lidia's eyes were teary. "Nothing. Sometimes saying you're sorry is not enough." She maneuvered around Sydney.

"So, this is it? You don't want to be a Nightingale anymore, so now I don't get to lead the group either?" Sydney asked, getting angry even though she was crying.

"You don't know that's what's going to happen," Lidia said.

"That's exactly what's going to happen!" Sydney cried. "If you give up your captain slot, Whitney and Micayla are going to try to oust me. I'll never survive if one of them gets co-captain with me. They won't stop till it's the two of them. The group is already a mess."

"You don't even have a group at the moment," Lidia fired back. "You think you're too good for any of my picks."

Sydney almost laughed. "Puppet Girl? You just want her to make me mad."

"I don't need Puppet Girl to make you mad." Lidia wiped her eyes. "But you know what? This is no longer my problem." Lidia walked down the stairs.

"Wait!" Sydney's voice cracked. "If they take over, the Nightingales will be finished. You *know* that. Is that really what you want?"

Lidia stopped walking but she didn't turn around. "You can't blame me for this. You did this to yourself. Good-bye, Sydney."

120

Sydney stopped talking. She knew she wouldn't change Lidia's mind, but she couldn't walk away. She waited till Lidia was no longer visible before the tears started to come faster and she audibly sobbed.

Lidia had stepped down as co-captain.

The Nightingales didn't have enough members. Even if they got them, Micayla and Whitney would probably stage a coup and steal the group.

But worst of all?

Sydney had lost her best friend.

Gabby might have been onto something: Sophomore year was definitely cursed.

CHAPTER THIRTEEN

Julianna

What word rhymed with "free"?

Let's go and *see*?

Nah.

Time for a spending *spree*?

When did she ever go on a spending spree? She crossed out both sentences.

A chance to be *me*?

Yes.

Julianna quickly scribbled the new line in her notebook, trying to keep up with the thoughts.

When a song idea came on, she stopped, dropped, and wrote. She preferred to be in front of her piano at home or have her guitar, but she was waiting for her first Nightingales practice to start so she had neither. As she sat in one of the back rows of the theater, she used her knees as a makeshift desk and the sound of the other Nightingales talking as her background music. Julianna looked down at her note-book and reread the last stanza she'd written.

After years of being shackled to the me I thought I should be,
Now I'm finally free,
The chains are gone, the scars remain,
But I won't let them continue to reign,
I'm free to be the me I was always meant to be.

The lyrics actually weren't terrible. They were much better than her ode to late-night french fries that was written on the opposite page. *(Drop me in the deep fryer! Just the sound makes my stomach feel like it's on fire.)*

It really didn't matter what she wrote. Sometimes the hardest thing a writer could do was write. After Julianna got the Sounds of the Future songwriting contest rejection the week before, she was sure she'd never pick up a pen again. She envisioned a bonfire where she burned all her lyrics and idea books. But Sydney's invitation to join the Nightingales had changed all that. It gave her some faith in herself.

Whether she could actually get up on a stage and sing in front of people was a different story.

Julianna heard someone talking at the speed of light and looked up. Gabby was walking toward her.

"Do we know who else is going to be here? Is Lidia coming? Are they still fighting? I haven't seen them together all week. Has anyone heard anything? Vi? Vi, are you listening to me? Vi?" Gabby poked the girl listening to music on her headphones. "VI!"

Viola slid off the headphones and let them rest on her neck. "What?"

"Hey! It's you!" Gabby said, stopping short when she saw Julianna staring. "What are you doing here?"

"I came back to audition and I made the group," Julianna said shyly, leaving out the details of her audition. "You guys too?"

"Yes." Gabby counted heads in the room as Viola slipped her headphones on again and started singing to herself. Her voice was really layered. "And good for you! I guess that means there really are enough girls for a group."

Julianna frowned. "What do you mean?"

"Didn't you hear?" Gabby asked. "The pool of talent was so small, Sydney had to take basically everyone who tried out. We're lucky we've gotten enough girls to compete."

Julianna's stomach felt funny. "Everyone?"

Was that the real reason Sydney had picked her? Because she was forced to?

Viola removed her headphones yet again, hearing Julianna's thoughts. "I wouldn't sweat it. I'm sure you're good. Would you have tried out for the group if you weren't?" Someone called Viola's name, and Gabby spotted someone she knew too and rushed off talking a mile a minute.

Julianna sat in the auditorium seat in stunned silence. Was she a pity invite?

Her phone started to ring and she pulled it out of her bag. It was Amy. She quickly answered it. Maybe the call would take her mind off things. "Hey."

"Ju-Ju!" Amy shouted, her voice as big and bright as if she were sitting next to her. "Sorry I haven't been in touch this week. I've been slammed. How's that fancy school treating you?"

"I like it," Julianna admitted to herself as much as to Amy.

The girls onstage had started to sing a Beyoncé song. They sounded good, which was a relief to Julianna. Maybe they weren't pity invites.

"Do I hear singing?" Amy asked. "Where are you?"

"I'm in the school theater," Julianna said, sitting up straight in the seat, which squeaked. "I have some news."

"Me too," Amy said. "Me first! Guess who made captain of the Tonal Teens? Me!" She screamed so loud, Julianna had to hold the phone away from her ear.

"Whoa, that's amazing!" Amy was only a sophomore, but people in the group adored her. "I have some news too," Julianna said shyly. She'd been dying to tell Amy, but this was bigger than a text. "Guess who made the girls' a cappella team at Bradley? Me!" Julianna waited to hear Amy's reaction.

There was none.

"Did you hear me?" Julianna asked, putting her hand over her other ear so she could hear. The Beyoncé song was getting loud. She looked at her phone to see if the call had been dropped. "Amy? Did I lose you?"

"No! Sorry. You made the Nightingales?" Amy's voice sounded odd. "That's great, Ju-Ju! They must really need new blood this year."

Julianna squirmed. Amy couldn't have meant it the way it sounded. "What do you mean?"

"Oh my God, Ju-Ju, I'm sorry," Amy said, laughing. "I just meant you didn't make the Tonal Teens that one time you tried out, and I never hear you sing so I'm just surprised, that's all."

Double ouch. "I know I didn't make the Tonal Teens, but I do sing," Julianna said defensively. *In the shower.*

"Well, you must if you got up the nerve to try out," Amy added. "You threw me! I guess I didn't expect you to try out for an a cappella group."

"A music group elective is a requirement here," Julianna said, but she felt funny explaining herself, as if she had to justify why she was now singing a cappella.

"This means we're going to be competitors now," Amy said. Amy didn't sound happy about that.

"Maybe this means we'll get to see each other at a competition," Julianna suggested. "That would be fun."

"Yeah, fun," Amy said. "Listen, I have to go. Captain duty calls. Talk to you soon!" She hung up before Julianna could even say good-bye.

That was bizarre. What was up with Amy? Julianna made a mental note to talk to Naya later and see if anything was going on. She closed her notebook and headed toward the other girls, who were still warming up. Gabby ran over to her.

"Guys? This is Julianna. She's new!" Gabby threw her arms around her. "Julianna, the team."

A small group of girls said—or sang—hello.

"Shouldn't Sydney and Lidia be here to make the introductions?" a pretty girl with wavy hair said. "You'd think the captains would get here early to welcome us."

"Chill, Whitney. I'm sure they're on their way." Viola quickly made introductions. There was Mercedes, a girl who spoke as loud as someone wearing headphones. A girl named Donna had a puppet drawn on her fist.

"This is Ms. Heel," Donna explained. "Hello!" the puppet said.

"Your fist has a *name*?" Micayla asked, looking at the others. "Are we being pranked? There is no way a puppet is a Nightingale."

"Micayla," Viola said, sounding a lot like a mother, which seemed to suit her. She had a calming way about her that put Julianna at ease. "Sydney and Lidia know what they want for this group. I'm sure Ms. Heel will fit right in." She winked at Donna.

"It wouldn't work in *my* group," Micayla muttered.

That anxious feeling Julianna was trying to ignore was creeping back.

"Four, five, six, seven, eight." Whitney counted the girls. She had the reddest lips Julianna had ever seen. They were glossed to a high-test sheen. "Wait a minute. Who's missing? There's only nine of us and we need ten. Who's number ten?"

"Actually, we need two more to form a group," said Sydney as she walked down the ramp with a huge box that had pink wigs sticking out of it.

Everyone started talking at once, a flurry of questions being shouted over one another. Viola and Sydney tried to keep everyone calm, but it didn't work. Sydney finally whistled loudly and everyone stopped talking.

"As I was saying, we need two more members." She frowned. "We have to have at least ten to compete."

Whitney motioned to the small group. "You're telling me everyone who tried out got a slot?"

Sydney's cheeks colored. "Pretty much." Everyone started talking again. "But that doesn't mean you didn't deserve to be here! We're lucky we had such talent show up." She pushed her blond hair behind her right ear. "Now we just have to work on fine-tuning everyone's talents a little bit and possibly finding a new member. Fast."

"Where's Lidia?" Micayla asked, a small smile playing on her lips.

Julianna looked from Gabby to Viola to Sydney. Did everyone know something the others didn't?

Sydney looked down at the box she was still holding. "She's not coming." There was an awkward pause. "Lidia decided to leave the group."

The uproar started up again. Everyone was talking so loud, Julianna couldn't hear a word Sydney was trying to say.

"Listen!" Sydney shouted at the top of her lungs and everyone got quiet again. "Geez. I have to stop screaming or I'm going to damage my vocal cords."

"Lidia's gone?" Whitney asked again.

"Yes. She's already talked to Mr. Wickey, so it's a done deal. There's no changing her mind so don't even bother trying." Sydney wouldn't make eye contact with them. "She wants to do other extra-curriculars this year and I'm happy for her. Really."

The group was quiet.

"So it's got nothing to do with you kissing Griffin Mancini?" Whitney asked and Sydney's cheeks colored.

Micayla tsked. "Kingfisher and Nightingale hookups are frowned upon. You know that."

"This has nothing to do with a guy," Sydney said. Julianna had a feeling there was more to the story. "If Lidia doesn't want us, then we don't want her. People should be here because they want to be Nightingales."

"Like me!" someone said and they all turned around.

Pearl Robbins was running down the aisle, her hair bouncing wildly. She practically tackled Sydney. "I heard you are short members. I know I didn't make the cut again, but please, please, please let me try out again."

Whitney and Micayla snickered.

Julianna bit her lip. She'd heard Pearl sing. She was pitchy. Could they help her with that so she could make the group? Julianna had no idea.

"Pearl," Sydney started to say.

"No! Listen," Pearl begged. "I tried to sing at auditions, but I have another talent that I was afraid to show you." She bit her lip. "There is something I've gotten good at this summer." She looked at the others. "You see, I love the Pentatonix and I've been watching them a lot and learning how to do percussion sounds. Anyway, Vi says I'm good so . . ."

"You're rambling! Good at what?" snapped Whitney. "This is an a cappella group. You need to be able to sing. You better not have a puppet too!" Everyone started bickering again.

"Hey! Let the girl talk," said Viola, popping gum into her mouth. "She's really good at what she does. Show them, Pearl."

Pearl suddenly seemed shy. "I learned how to beatbox."

Sydney's right eyebrow went up. "Beatbox. We haven't had one of those in a few years." She sounded sort of excited.

"I learned it this year." Pearl shifted awkwardly. "If you give me a song, and someone agrees to sing, I can show you how I do it."

Whitney and Micayla stepped back as if they couldn't be bothered, but Viola raised her hand.

"I'll sing and you do your thing," Viola told her.

"This is a waste of time," Micayla said. "She can't sing. She auditioned already."

"Guys, we need more members and we don't have a beatboxer. Let's give her a chance." Sydney took a seat on the arm of one of the auditorium chairs. "Pearl, let's hear what you've got."

Pearl whispered something to Viola, who nodded. Then Viola started to sing a Drake song they were all familiar with. One stanza in, Pearl came in, but she wasn't singing lyrics. She was making sounds. Her mouth was clicking, her tongue was moving, and the noises she was making sounded like instruments. Pearl's mouth was like a symphony with percussion instruments and every sound was coming out of this one tiny girl.

When she was done, everyone seemed momentarily stunned. Julianna was the first to clap. Others joined in and finally Sydney stood up and bear-hugged her.

"That was . . . that was . . ." She couldn't seem to find the words. "OMG, that was amazing! How did you learn that arrangement?"

Pearl shrugged. "I didn't. I just listen to the music over and over and come up with something that works for each song."

"And you'd be willing to work out arrangements with me for all our songs?" Sydney asked. Pearl nodded. "You'll have to show Mr. Wickey too just to make it official, but I say you're in! Welcome to the Nightingales!"

Everyone, even Whitney and Micayla, applauded.

"Aww, a group hug!" said Dave as he and the Kingfishers burst into the auditorium talking loudly. "What are you guys doing? Saying good-bye, since you don't have enough members for a group?"

"We do too have a group," Sydney said indignantly and looked at her phone to check the time. "And what are you guys doing here? We have this space today."

"Do you?" Pasqual feigned innocence. "I thought we had it on Tuesdays. Or was that Wednesdays?" He shrugged. "Well, we're here now and unlike you guys, we're already working on arrangements. Our Ed Sheeran track is on fire and we need to lay it down today. So if you girls are just chatting . . ."

"Which Ed Sheeran song?" Sydney sounded suspicious.

"The new one," said Dave.

"That Ed Sheeran song is on our list," said Sydney. "I already submitted it to Mr. Wickey for approval."

Dave stepped forward. "So did I. When did you hand it in?"

Sydney waved her arms wildly. "Today."

"So did I," said Dave. "What time?"

"Two p.m. You?"

"Two p.m."

They glared at each other as the entire stage went "Ooh."

"What's happening?" Julianna whispered to the other girls as Dave and Sydney stared each other down.

"It's an a cappella showdown," said Whitney excitedly. "No two groups can submit the same song for the same season. If they both want it, it goes to the team that submitted it first, but if they both submitted it at the same time then there is a sing-off to see who sings it better." She looked around. "Mr. Wickey is usually the tiebreaker and he's not here."

Julianna's heart started to pound. She was going to have to sing this afternoon? In front of *both* a cappella groups? She thought of Amy's reaction again and the fact that the Nightingales barely had enough girls to form a team, and her old insecurities started to creep up on her. Did she even belong up on that stage?

Dave opened his arms wide. "Let's do this, Nightingales. Tell you what? We're gentlemen. We'll even let you go first." The guys started to cheer.

"Fine!" Sydney declared and looked defiantly at her group. She called them over to a huddle. "We *have* to win this," she told them. "It will be too hard to harmonize when we don't all know the lyrics yet. Does everyone know the chorus?" The girls nodded.

"I can beatbox," Pearl said.

"Great!" Sydney nodded.

"Whit and I sing this all the time in the car," Micayla said. "We can handle the harmony."

"Excellent!" Sydney said. "We just need a strong singer to anchor the rest of the song."

They all looked at Viola.

"You know I don't do singer-songwriter types." Viola sounded insulted. "I don't know this tune."

"Neither does Ms. Heel," said Donna. "She prefers hard rock."

"Same," said Gabby.

Sydney's eyes landed on Julianna. Her heart did another flip and her throat suddenly felt like it was on fire.

"Do you know the lyrics?" Sydney asked.

"Kind of," Julianna said, "but . . ."

"Thank God." Sydney yanked her onto the stage. "Let's go."

"Sing it, Nightingales!" one of the guys teased.

Julianna suddenly felt dizzy. The lights onstage felt too bright, the air too warm. Everyone's voices were magnifying. Oh no. It was happening again. She was getting stage fright!

"Sydney, I'm not feeling that great," Julianna tried to tell her, but her voice came out muffled.

Sydney grabbed her by the shoulders and smiled. "You're going to do great! Your voice is insane! Get us this song! We need this!" She pushed Julianna toward the front of the stage.

She could see the guys lined up in front, whistling and shouting taunts.

Julianna was certain. She was going to pass out on the stage and fall off. Would anyone catch her? Her mouth was so dry. What was happening? *Keep it together, Julianna. You can do this! Sing!*

Pearl started beatboxing. Whitney and Micayla added in a harmony. Finally, it was Julianna's turn. *Sing!* she told herself. She looked at Dave, who was laughing. Julianna opened her mouth, but suddenly she felt like she was going to throw up. She glanced worriedly back at Sydney, who was wildly motioning for her to start.

"You've got this, Julianna!" Gabby cheered.

Julianna closed her eyes, took a deep breath, and something happened. Her phone was vibrating. She was saved!

"It's my mom!" she said, looking at the screen. Her eyes were so blurry she had no clue who the message was from, but it didn't matter. "I need to . . . some sort of emergency . . . can't stay . . . I've got to take this!" Julianna stuttered, and hurried offstage to pretend to take the call.

"Julianna, wait!" Sydney tried.

Julianna could hear the Kingfishers cheering at her absence. She had definitely cost the Nightingales the song. Her face burned as she thought about the humiliation, but she tried not to make herself crazy. She moved far into the back of the stage area where she couldn't be seen in the darkness and finally looked at her phone screen.

AMY: Sorry if I was weird before. Too much caffeine!

AMY: Congrats on getting in. With you in the group, I'm sure the Florida a cappella scene is going to go (Lady) gaga over the Nightingales!

CHAPTER FOURTEEN

Sydney

"Wait! Where are you going?" Sydney watched in horror as her group's newest star ran offstage to take a phone call. Sydney knew stage fright when she saw it. How had she not seen the signs before? Julianna hadn't missed the original audition. She had panicked then too. She could go after her, but there was no way she was getting her on that stage to sing Sheeran right now.

"Who takes a phone call in the middle of a performance?" Whitney asked, clearly annoyed as she watched Dave and Pasqual high-five.

"You owe me ten bucks," Dave told Pasqual. "Told you that girl would choke again."

"She didn't choke!" Sydney covered for her. "She just had an important call."

"She kind of choked," Gabby whispered just to Sydney and Viola. "She made an excuse during the auditions too. I thought you knew that."

Sydney looked at the spot Julianna had originally been standing in and sighed. "Well, I do now."

"Poor girl," said Viola. "Someone should go talk to her. I'll find her."

"No, give her space," Sydney said. "I don't want to scare her off completely." They needed warm bodies.

The most talented girl on the squad couldn't handle singing in public. This was just great! Sydney closed her eyes and tried to breathe. *Everything will be fine.*

"Syd? You okay?" Griffin asked.

Griffin. She couldn't do this right now. "Can we start from the top with a new soloist?" Sydney asked, not looking in his direction.

"Do-over?" Dave sputtered. "No way. You had your shot. Now it's our turn."

Sydney bit her lip.

"Great work, leader." Micayla patted Sydney on the shoulder as they filed off the stage.

The guys stood in their classic triangle formation with Dave at the front. Griffin was to his right and Pasqual to his left. They bowed their heads, pressed their palms together like they were praying, and waited. They had two beatboxers who kicked the song off before Griffin's voice came roaring in followed by Dave, who rapped. They performed the tune as if they had done it a hundred times before.

"No fair," Gabby whined. "They've definitely practiced this already."

"Of course, they've rehearsed already," Whitney said, hitting Sydney where it hurt.

Gabby shook her head. "The Nightingales' curse strikes again."

By the end of the song, Sydney knew there was no contest. The Kingfishers were the clear victors, but she still wasn't willing to give up her shot. She begged for another chance to perform, promising at the end of the song they'd agree to pick one winner even without Mr. Wickey's presence.

She huddled with her teammates—minus one—again. "We're going to be okay," she said, even if she didn't feel that way. Her eyes were as wild as her curly hair, which had lost its taming headband. "We can beat them without Julianna." She looked at the group and pulled them in tight. "Whitney and Micayla, you kick off the first stanza; Gabby and Viola, you do the melody; Pearl, you beatbox; and . . ." She hesitated when she came to Mercedes and Donna. "You two can join me on the chorus. Keep your voices low so we don't overpower the others." Mercedes, Donna, and Ms. Heel nodded.

"I'm not sure of the lyrics," Gabby said. "Can I hold up my phone and read them?"

"We can't hold our phones during a performance," Micayla protested.

"Do we have a choice?" Viola asked.

"WHY DON'T WE SING THE SONG IN A ROUND! I'LL START!" said Mercedes in the only volume she seemed to have—extra-loud.

"A round? Those are lame!" Whitney exclaimed.

"*Real* a cappella groups don't do them anymore," Micayla added. "Unless you're talking about the Tonal Teens. They do them, but they can do anything because they're state champs."

"Instead of the chorus, can Ms. Heel have her own part?" Donna asked.

"Let's stick with the plan," said Sydney, trying to get their attention back. The girls turned to the stage to perform.

Sydney quickly regretted that decision.

Pearl started beatboxing but kept getting drowned out by Mercedes, who sang at the top of her lungs. Donna's puppet hit Gabby in the face when she attempted a spin. Sydney looked at the Kingfishers. One was videoing the Nightingales' epic fail on his phone. Others were laughing. This was humiliating. Sydney had to end this.

"You guys win," Sydney said, even though they still had half a song left to sing.

"What? We didn't even finish yet!" Whitney complained.

"We didn't have an arrangement," Sydney said. "They clearly already had one. They should get the Sheeran song." Dave hopped up onstage and shook her hand. Sydney wouldn't let go. She looked him straight in the eyes. "You get the arrangement, but *we* get the theater." Dave's face fell. "I *know* I booked Tuesdays. Stop trying to mess with us."

"Fine. Better luck next time." Dave winked. "I'm sure there's a lot of great songs out there that we haven't claimed yet. Not." He and some of the others laughed.

She waited till the guys were gone to collapse onto the stage. The others plopped down next to her.

She'd had such big dreams for the Nightingales and they included that Sheeran song. She'd been working on an arrangement already, but that arrangement hinged on Lidia, who was going to tackle a tricky solo. Just the thought of Lidia made her blood boil. How could she do this to her? Dropping out of the group because of a boy? How could she do this to the group?

"So when are you going to pick a new co-captain?" Micayla asked, playing with her chunky beaded necklace. "Because the Nightingales and Kingfishers have always had two."

Whitney sat up on her knees. Her blue eyes were gleaming. "Do we apply to Mr. Wickey? If so, I want to go now so I can get my name in first."

"Whit! I just said I was applying!" Micayla pouted.

"We can both apply!" Whitney told her and the two of them looked at each other as if a new thought had occurred to them. It was one Sydney was already worried about.

She was not getting ousted! She would make this team work! She'd teach Mercedes to sing softer and Donna to lose the puppet. She'd duct-tape Julianna's feet to the stage floor so she couldn't run. She'd find another member *if* they needed one. Sydney stood up. "I don't need another co-captain," she declared.

"What?" everyone said.

Sydney's voice was firm. "I am telling Mr. Wickey I don't need another co-captain."

"He's not going to listen," Whitney said, but Sydney didn't care.

"Syd, it's a lot of work," Viola said. "Don't you need help?"

Sydney ran her hand through her hair again, making it wild, and blinked as she stared off at the theater lights. Lidia may have been more organized, and the calmer of the two of them, but Sydney had one captain trait that Lidia didn't: She wasn't a quitter.

"I'll be fine," Sydney told them, her eyes blazing. "We're going to be the best Nightingales team Bradley has ever had! It's going to be an amazing season!" She threw her fist in the air and cheered. No one joined her.

"What should we do about Julianna?" Gabby asked.

"I'll talk to her tomorrow. For now—" She patted her notebook. "We have plenty of songs to choose from. Great songs!" Sydney looked at the girls. "Text your parents and tell them you're not making the late bus. We are holding a three-hour meeting to pick songs and then we're going to submit them to Mr. Wickey tonight!"

Viola stood up and put an arm around Sydney. "That seems like a lot to do in one day. Why don't we concentrate on one song and try to figure out harmonies? Didn't you bring a box of pink stuff you wanted to show us?"

"Ah! My magic!" Sydney squealed, running over to the box forgotten about on the floor. "The Kingfishers made me forget. I downloaded a montage of winning a cappella group videos to show you guys as inspiration. Then I thought we'd kick off the practice with a fun improv a cappella number set to someone we'd normally never cover like the Fidget Femmes. That's why I brought these pink wigs, boas, and light-up sunglasses."

"Is this an a cappella group or did we join the circus?" Micayla asked.

Sydney put on a pair of glasses and lit them up. "An a cappella group. Now come on."

The girls all reached into the box and came out with wigs, boas, and sunglasses.

"Mine doesn't fit right."

"My glasses are broken!"

"I think I'm allergic to this boa."

"Why do we have to sing with props? The Nightingales never use props!"

They were talking over one another again and it was hard to concentrate with so much noise. "Come on, guys!" Sydney tried. "Just go with it! It's time to face the music!"

Everyone looked at one another. Then they burst out in song.

"Turn up the music, turn it up now! Let it move you, move you now!" they sang to one another. Pearl came in and beatboxed while the group continued singing through a second and third verse of the popular Fidget Femmes song before finally stopping.

Sydney looked at the group in awe. "That sounded good!"

"It sounded hella amazing!" Viola said.

Sydney agreed. Who needed Lidia?

This was going to require serious work, but no one was taking the Nightingales away from her.

CHAPTER FIFTEEN

Lidia

Her legs felt like they were on fire. Her brow was beaded with sweat, her pink leotard reeked, and they hadn't had a water break in a half hour. To prepare for her competition team tryout, Lidia had been taking several classes every day that week. She was quickly learning Miss Pattie Ann showed no sign of quitting even if Lidia's fitness tracker said there were only ten minutes left of class. Lidia breathed heavily. Shouldn't they be cooling down instead of doing continuous fouetté turns in front of the wall-length mirror?

"People, you call that full-out?" Miss Pattie Ann asked as the last dancer finished her turns. Lidia had only managed four, but she hadn't fallen or collapsed on the floor so she considered that a win. There were people in her class who had done ten continuous spins.

"Some of you looked like you were sleepwalking." Miss Pattie Ann walked the line where the dancers held their finished poses until they were told not to. "Hmm . . . I know you need to get to your next class, but I'm thinking we need another turn across the floor."

Across the floor again? Water, she needed water!

Miss Pattie Ann queued up a change of music on her iPhone. "Let's try some a la seconde turns, followed by four pirouettes and a tour jeté jump."

Tour jeté jumps were Lidia's kryptonite. Miss Pattie Ann may have thought Lidia was ready to try out for the senior competition team, but Lidia was quickly realizing she had a lot of work to do if she was going to make it. The summer intensive classes were tough, but competition classes were grueling daily workouts that lasted hours. She'd been at the studio for two hours already and she had to work twice as hard as everyone else to keep up with simple routines they already knew.

The great thing about dance was, it kept her mind off everything going on at school.

That day in Mr. Wickey's office had been the low point. Seeing Sydney and Griffin singing at the piano cemented her belief that Sydney and Griffin's kiss was no accident. Sydney liked him and he liked her, and Lidia couldn't handle watching them fall for each other. She had to get away from it all, and the only place she could do that was at the studio. She'd thrown herself into classes this week, doing jeté turns and floor routines around the clock. Slowly, her mood started to change. She couldn't wait to get off the bus and into the studio, which was buzzing with students. She loved wrapping up the ribbons on her pointe shoes, wearing hip-hop boots, or just dancing barefoot. And her favorite part was how no one knew she was part of an "a cappella scandal" because her best friend had fallen for the guy she liked. At dance, she was just Lidia, aspiring competition team member.

She loved that. Even if there were moments when she felt guilty.

Lidia may have been mad at Sydney, but she wasn't mad at the Nightingales, and she was starting to see there was a difference. After Sydney told the group Lidia had quit, some of the Nightingales had been reaching out.

"Come back! Sydney needs you! The team can't work without you!" Gabby and Viola said, filling her with stories about how the Kingfishers swiped Syd's favorite Ed Sheeran song, how they weren't sure they had enough members to compete, and how the infighting among Whitney, Sydney, and Micayla was ramping up. Lidia had been looking forward to singing that Sheeran song (especially since the arrangement they came up with gave her a great solo). Lidia could just picture Sydney unconsciously pushing her hair behind her ears and trying to sound upbeat like a cheerleader, trying to keep the group together. If the Nightingales crashed and burned, Sydney would be lost at Bradley and it would kind of be Lidia's fault.

Miss Pattie Ann clapped in time to the rhythm, bringing Lidia back to the present. *Sydney is not my problem anymore*, she told herself. *She was a terrible friend and karma caught up with her.*

But if that's true, why do I still feel so guilty about the Nightingales?

The music switched tempo again and the volume shot up. Lidia's toes started tapping in time to the music.

She may not have known what to do about Sydney or the Nightingales, but she did know how to dance.

Twenty minutes later, she got her water break. If she hurried, she'd make the 5:50 p.m. bus home and be halfway through her precalculus homework before dinner. She made her way down the hall to grab her dance bag.

"Lidia?"

She turned around. Miss Pattie Ann's head was sticking out of one of the studio doors. She could hear the music pumping behind the door and the giggles from younger students.

"Nice job today," Miss Pattie Ann said appraisingly. "You're keeping up. I think you're ready for your audition."

Lidia's heart did a fouetté turn. Miss Pattie Ann rarely paid compliments. She just pushed you harder. "I am ready. When is my audition?"

Miss Pattie Ann smiled. "How about this Friday at five?"

Friday I have Nightingales practice, she thought. She'd forgotten to take it off her iCalendar and the schedule kept popping up on her phone. *You used to have Nightingales practice*, she reminded herself. "Friday at five would be great. Thank you."

She officially had an audition for the senior competition dance team! This was cause for celebration! Lidia forgot all about the bus schedule and headed straight for Kyle's Candy Shoppe. She was envisioning a nonpareil in her mouth as she opened the store door.

"Hey, Lidia."

Lidia turned around, her ponytail smacking her in the face. She felt her heart stop. "Griffin." She sucked in her breath. "Hey."

"Hi." Griffin genuinely smiled as if he was happy to see her. He was leaning on the store window like he had no place to be but there.

Lidia took a snapshot of this image in her mind. His hazel eyes were magnetic, but it was his smile, with the small gap between his two lower teeth, and the way his face tanned leaving just a trace of freckles, that did her in. He was wearing an outrageous graphic tee, like he usually did outside of class, and had on board shorts. Syd had told her Griffin showed up at play practices in board shorts too, as if he'd just come from the beach. These ones had tacky pineapples on them.

"What are you doing here?" he asked.

"Getting candy," she said, nodding to the store she was about to enter before she saw him.

Griffin laughed. "I know that. I meant downtown."

"Oh." She blushed. "I take dance classes at Integral Dance down the block."

Griffin's face clouded over. "I heard you left the Nightingales."

Lidia paled. *Please don't ask me why.* "Yes. Not enough time to do everything I want to do," she joked. "I had to give something up."

"But the Nightingales?" Griffin questioned. "I thought you loved being in the group."

"I did." She stood up straighter, her hand closing over the top of her dance bag. She had to remind herself to breathe. "But like I said, not enough time." *Please don't ask me to say more. I don't want to talk about it. I hardly know you.*

The thought hit Lidia like an accidental dance kick to the stomach. *I hardly know you.* It was true, wasn't it? Everything she knew about Griffin was through Sydney. Sydney was the one who had gotten to know him. Here was her chance to connect with Griffin and she had no clue what to say. She didn't feel comfortable opening up to him, and she couldn't figure out how to make small talk either. He must have felt the same because he was quiet too. The sounds of the light street traffic grew louder as she racked her brain.

"I'm sure you're glad the play is over," Lidia blurted out. That wasn't what she meant. Why would he be happy to be done with *In the Heights*? Syd had said Griffin wanted their run of the show to go on forever. He was as much of a Broadway fanatic as she was. "I mean, so you can start thinking about the Naples Music Festival *and stuff*." What was it about Griffin that made her lose her head?

His mouth twisted awkwardly. He popped in a piece of peppermint gum. He was never without it. "Are you okay with that? Us doing the Naples Music Festival together, I mean?"

He knows I like him, Lidia realized. She'd walked right into this trap. "I'm fine," Lidia said quickly. "That's great you and Sydney were picked."

Griffin's face flooded with relief. "Oh good. I didn't want it to be weird."

This is already weird, Lidia thought and she couldn't help but smirk. "It's fine," she said again.

"Have you talked to her?" Griffin asked, his face hopeful. "She seems overwhelmed at practice without you."

"No, I haven't," Lidia said. *He really likes her.* She could see it now. "*He* kissed me," she remembered Sydney saying. She might have been telling the truth about that part. Lidia's grip on the doorknob tightened. "Well, I should run in and get that candy so I don't miss the bus."

"Yes," Griffin said. "I should go too. The Kingfishers have a working dinner practice." Griffin grinned. "We've got a reputation to uphold, you know."

So smug. For the first time ever, Lidia found herself wanting to get away from Griffin Mancini. "Have fun."

"You too," he said. "Nice talking to you, Lidia."

"You too too," Lidia said and realized she'd said "too" twice. Why? Why did he do this to her? And why was it so hard to talk to him?

"Why?" she found herself muttering as she yanked open the door to Kyle's and stepped inside. "You too *too*. Who says that? Have you talked to her? Who says that either?" she mumbled.

"Rough practice?" Kyle asked. He was standing on a stool refilling the soft-serve ice cream machine. Lidia resisted the urge to jump over the counter and chug the soft-serve vanilla by the gallon.

"I need nonpareils as if my life depended on it." She eyed a group of younger kids sitting at a table trading gummies. Sharks, worms, people, spiders. It's like they had their own personal game of poker going. They looked so happy. None of them looked like they had lost their a cappella friends, their best friend, and the guy they liked in just a few short weeks.

"You're in luck." Kyle placed a large plastic bag on the counter.

Lidia grabbed the bag and peeked inside. There had to be at least three pounds of nonpareils in there! There weren't just white-sprinkled ones either. There were multicolored and vanilla ones as well. She ripped open the bag and popped one into her mouth. Aaah . . . just what she needed.

Kyle leaned on the counter. "They're all yours. They've already been paid for." He handed her a note.

Lidia opened the small green card with the even smaller green piece of paper inside. There was a sketch of Sailor Moon on it.

Wanted to make sure you had chocolate to survive the week. ☺ Also, any chance you want to go with me to a cosplay gathering next Sunday? It's at the Naples Seaside Resort from 1-5 p.m. You'd be the best Sailor Moon in the place!—Jack.

"Jack," Lidia said aloud, unable to hide her smile. He'd bought her nonpareils and invited her out. Sure, it was to dress up in costume as her favorite comic character, but it still counted as a date, right? She thumbed Jack's phone number, which he had scribbled neatly at the bottom of the note.

"He came in yesterday before his class," Kyle told her. "He bought me out of nonpareils again." He shook his head. "I swear between the two of you, I'm going to need to start making more of these things."

"Do you think he's at class now?" Lidia asked, her heart thumping a little faster at the prospect of seeing Jack.

Kyle thought for a moment. "No, he doesn't go there on Tuesdays. He'll be there tomorrow, though. But give me a heads-up if you're going to be buying *him* nonpareils. I'll start making a batch now."

Lidia clutched the bag of chocolate and headed out. She was still smiling as she walked in her front door a half hour later. Her smile faded when she saw her mom sitting at the dining room table.

"You're home," Lidia said, and immediately started to feel uneasy. "I thought you'd be with Dougie at soccer practice."

"Your father took him," her mom said.

Lidia could see Grandma Evie in the kitchen singing "Bubble Gum Love" again. She had on a long print dress and double strands of necklaces wrapped around her neck. Her grandmother was always dressed to go out. "What if Bradley Cooper rings the bell and asks me to go out and I'm not ready?" she always said when Dougie or Lidia teased her about it.

"I wanted to be home early so we could talk before dinner," her mom said.

Lidia had been avoiding this conversation for days. "Okay."

"Talk in the kitchen so I can hear you!" Grandma Evie yelled. "This way I don't have to spy."

Lidia and her mom couldn't help but grin.

"Do you think Mariah Carey sings her old hits while she cooks?" Lidia teased as she followed her mom into the kitchen.

"I doubt Mariah even knows the words to her songs, but I know mine." Her grandmother hit a high note Lidia didn't even realize she could still hit. Her grandmother reached for her hand and Lidia's mom's hands. "Sing with me."

Lidia's mom jumped right in. The pair looked at Lidia.

This time Lidia didn't fight it. She knew the words. She even knew which harmony to take. Her grandmother went high and Lidia and her mom went low. Lidia matched the pair note for note as she stared into her grandmother's dark-brown eyes. Her mom was singing beautifully, but there was something about her voice that sounded sad.

"Nice," her grandmother said as they hit the last note together.

"Very nice for a girl who is no longer in a cappella." Lidia's smile faded as her mom and grandmother both gave her a look.

"You guys know I love to sing with you," Lidia said, taking a seat at the table, "but I had to make a choice and I picked dance. I told you there's no time to do both."

Her mom sat down too while her grandmother went back to stirring the pot on the stove. "But you were so excited about the Nightingales when you were named captain last June," her mom reminded her. "What changed?"

"I started dancing every day this summer and I fell in love with it," Lidia admitted. "Now I'm trying out for the competition team and if I really want to make it, I need to practice every day. And I'm still singing in the chorus." *Which doesn't practice every day.*

Grandma Evie and Lidia's mom looked at each other.

"I see," her mom said. "So this has nothing to do with you fighting with Sydney?"

"How do you know I had a fight with Sydney?" Lidia asked calmly.

Her mom gave her a look. "I am the headmistress. I do hear things. Plus, Syd practically lived in this house all summer. She hasn't been here once since before school started."

"Okay, we had a fight," Lidia said and they both sighed, "but that wasn't the reason I quit the group. I left the Nightingales because I wanted to dance more."

"Really?" her mom pressed.

"Really!" Lidia insisted, but her voice sounded weaker. *And there's also part of me that's happy to be away from the drama.*

The two stared each other down.

Lidia finally looked at her grandmother. She was shaking her head, her earrings swinging. "Grandma Evie? What do you think about all this?"

"You have to do what makes you happy," her grandmother said. "For me, it's song. For you, it's dance, right?"

"Yes," she gushed. "My teacher pushes me to be better than I think I can be, and I love having the time now to take so many different classes."

"But?" her grandmother and mother asked.

They knew her too well.

"Part of me feels like I let the Nightingales down," Lidia admitted.

"I knew it!" her mom said happily. "You miss the group!"

"Of course she misses the group," Grandma Evie said. "They were a family. Even if many of the girls are new this year, the group was her home for the last few years. When you move away, you always miss home. That doesn't mean you go running back."

Her mom sank back into her chair. She looked like a kid. "True." She grabbed Lidia's hand. "If dance is what makes you happy, I won't keep harping on it. I was just worried about you. I don't even know if the Nightingales have enough girls to have a team anyway . . ." She trailed off and squeezed Lidia's hand again. "It's not your problem."

Lidia felt a pang of guilt again. "Can't they perform with fewer girls? Did you appeal to the a cappella board for them? What did Mr. Wickey say? Did Sydney think about hosting new tryouts? Is that allowed? The Nightingales can't just disappear!" she said shrilly.

Grandma Evie started to hum another song Lidia remembered from her album.

Her mom was looking at her strangely. "We have it covered. Do you know Pearl? She just auditioned for beatboxer. She's really good. I think they'll be able to compete by adding one girl, and Mr. Wickey said they just met with one. "

"Pearl beatboxes?" Lidia asked.

Her mom nodded. "I heard her the other day. She's excellent. The rest of the team needs work. I think one girl has terrible stage fright. Sydney said she ran offstage at practice the other day."

Lidia had heard about this. It was Julianna, the same girl who freaked out the first morning of school when she was handed the mic.

"But again, not your problem. Sydney will get the team there." Her mom smiled. "I should go finish up some calls before dinner. I'm glad we talked." She stood up and kissed Lidia on the head.

It's not your problem. Then why did Lidia feel like it was?

She reached for a piece of chocolate and her hand landed on Jack's note. She opened the card and looked for Jack's number. Then she texted him.

Thx for the chocolate. You convinced me. See you next
Sun. at 1 p.m.

She saw the typing bubbles pop up immediately. The reply came right back.

Hi, Ms. Nonpareils. Great. See you then—if not before at
Kyle's.

CHAPTER SIXTEEN

Julianna

Julianna read Sydney's text again to be sure she had it right.

> Meet me at the mall at 5 p.m. on Friday and bring
> your dog!

Who brought their dog to the mall?

Apparently, a lot of people in Naples, because when Julianna arrived at the mall with Cocoa in tow, almost everyone had a dog with them. Then she saw the sign draped across a walkway: BARKY HOURS, FRIDAYS AT 5 P.M.! Everywhere Julianna looked, stores had water bowls and treats for four-legged guests. A young family with a double stroller had a Yorkie while a retiree held tight to a Great Dane. Cocoa barked happily as she encountered each pup, but Julianna felt anxious. Even though she'd been sitting with Sydney, Gabby, and Viola at lunch for the last week, no one had brought up the elephant in the room: Julianna's flake-out. She couldn't keep making excuses to leave the stage or run out whenever it was her turn to sing. Julianna wondered if this was why Sydney wanted to meet up today. Maybe she was cutting her from the group.

But if that was the case, why did she want her to bring Cocoa?

"Julianna!" Sydney was waving to her from a bench between a pretzel stand and an electronics store. Cocoa bolted for Sydney while Julianna held on tight. The hyper puppy loved any chance to meet new people.

"Who's this?" Sydney asked, dropping to her knees to pet Cocoa, who practically jumped in Sydney's lap as she slobbered all over her.

"Cocoa," Julianna said, pulling on the leash to get the puppy to sit. "Cocoa, um, Krispy." The girls looked at each other and both burst out laughing. "Cheesy, I know." Julianna's face flushed. "But when we got her at the animal shelter this summer, it was the first thing I thought of. With her coloring, the name seemed to fit. Plus, it's my favorite cereal."

"It *is* a pretty good cereal." Sydney scratched Cocoa behind the ears. "If you're not partial to regular krispies like I am."

"She likes you," Julianna observed as Cocoa tried to eat Sydney's hair, "which is why you're one of the few people I've told her full name."

"Your secret is safe with me, Cocoa," Sydney told the dog. She looked up at Julianna. "So is yours, you know."

Julianna sat down. She pulled a squeaky toy shaped like a pine-apple out of her bag and threw it to Cocoa. "I should have told you about the stage fright. I thought I had it under control, but obviously, it's still a thing." She looked anxiously at Sydney. "I understand if you need to cut me from the group."

"Cut you?" Sydney looked baffled. "I brought you here to tell you about how badly we *need* you! I didn't want to bring this up at school in front of the others, but I hope you know you're the strongest vocalist I have. You're not going anywhere."

Julianna felt relief wash over her. So Sydney did like her voice. "Really?"

"Yes!" Sydney declared. "I have big plans for you, Ramirez. We just need to teach you to get on a stage and not want to run."

Julianna grabbed the squeaky toy from Cocoa and squeezed it. "I want you to know I wasn't always like this. I wanted to be in this a cappella group at my old high school—the Tonal Teens. I tried out and didn't make it."

"You tried out for the Tonal Teens and didn't make the cut?" Sydney asked in surprise. "There must be some talent pool at your old school if you didn't get in. Your voice is incredible."

"Thanks." Julianna blushed. "After that happened, I was so bummed, I stopped singing anywhere but at home. I didn't feel like my voice was worthy." Sydney huffed. "So I started writing songs that other people with better voices could sing and I love it. Not that I'm that good at writing tunes either."

"Why do you say that?" Sydney asked.

"I've entered three songwriting contests this year and never even won an honorable mention." Julianna shrugged. "I guess I'm not cut out for a career in music, but at Bradley that doesn't matter. Everyone has to do something. That's how I wound up trying out for the Nightingales. Headmistress Sato insisted."

Sydney nodded. "She was an original Nightingale, so she's our biggest fan and we're lucky to have her. She got the board to agree to let us perform with only nine girls this season now that Pearl is official." She put an arm around Julianna. "Which is why I need you on that stage! You're going to be electric up there." Julianna wasn't convinced. "I'm telling you, once you get over that fear, being onstage is more exciting than you can imagine. Hearing the crowd cheer and people applauding for you." Sydney closed her eyes. "There's no better feeling in the world."

"But what if they boo you?" Julianna said fearfully. "Or you hit a wrong note or miss a step or skip a word? There are so many things that can go wrong when you're onstage."

Sydney grabbed her friend by the shoulders. "You have to stop thinking so much! Just let it go and sing. When you sing in the shower, you don't prepare music first, do you?" Julianna shook her head. "Singing out loud can be as easy as walking down the street— you feel the music move you and break into song." Seated, she danced around on the bench. "Listen to the band playing right now," she instructed.

They were performing a cover of a Lyrica song that everyone was singing that fall. Sydney stood up and sang the song at the top of her lungs and didn't seem to care who heard her. *"You keep me spinning like a top, and I never want to stop, but the world stops, stops, stops, when I see you!"*

Cocoa barked her approval. "Thanks, Cocoa." Sydney bowed. "See? Easy! Try it!"

"Now? *At the mall?*" Alarm bells rang in Julianna's head. She started sliding away on the bench, pulling Cocoa, but Cocoa wouldn't budge. She dug in her heels and lay down. *Thanks a lot, pal,* Julianna thought.

Sydney grabbed Julianna's arm and helped her stand up. "It's an *outdoor mall*. No one is even looking at you! It's the perfect place to practice."

Julianna wasn't convinced. The crowds were thicker than they had been a few minutes earlier. There were more families. More kids. There were too many people who could hear her.

"Let's try this next week when I'm dressed better and have music with me that I like," Julianna said. She tried to leave and Sydney grabbed her. Cocoa looked back and forth between the girls and started to whine. She probably thought they were finally going for a walk.

"Watch me first," Sydney said. *"You keep me spinning like a top, and I never want to stop, but the world stops, stops, stops, when I see you!"*

A few people smiled, but others didn't even look up. "See? No one cares!" Sydney said. "The best part is we don't know anyone here! Look around." She pointed to people walking by. "That kid is drooling in his stroller, and the couple over there is helping each other with their hearing aids. This is the perfect place for you to sing. Half the crowd won't pay attention and the other half won't even hear you! Come on, you can do it!"

It was happening already. Her cheeks felt like they had sunburn. She started breathing heavily. Every sound around her magnified as if she were hearing them through a tunnel. She could hear Sydney's words over and over in her head: *No one is watching you. No one even cares!* But it wasn't working. She felt her brow start to sweat and her mouth go dry.

"I won't make you do it alone the first time, okay?" Sydney took Cocoa's leash from Julianna's hand, then hooked the leash around a tree branch next to the bench they were standing in front of. With Cocoa secure, she grabbed Julianna firmly and pulled her up on the bench. Julianna was sure she looked like a statue. Her body was rigid and her heartbeat sounded like it was being magnified by a megaphone. "Close your eyes if you want," Sydney instructed as she started swaying the two of them.

Julianna felt dizzy. "I'm going to fall."

"You're fine," Sydney said soothingly. "You look a little like wax, though. I'm going to ship you off to Ripley's after this performance." She laughed.

Julianna's laugh came out like a whisper. "Is there a statue for 'Girl Who Freaked Out at the Mall'?"

"No, but there's going to be one for 'Girl Gives Epic Performance at Barky Hour.'" Sydney grabbed Julianna's hand. "Look at me and only me."

"Not at the lady who just stopped in front of our bench and is staring at us as she eats her ice cream?" Julianna felt herself perspire.

"Don't look at her. Look at me."

Julianna looked at Sydney. Her eyes and her wide smile were so reassuring. Her breathing started to slow. It was just her and Sydney. No one else was there. She heard Sydney start to hum the song, which was coming up to the chorus. Julianna knew the words. They were on the tip of her tongue. Maybe she could really do this!

"Good!" Sydney encouraged her. "Just imagine we're two friends all alone singing to each other in the car."

It was the word "friends" that caught her attention. She and Amy used to sing in the car together. Amy, who had delivered the crushing news: You didn't make the Tonal Teens. Julianna hadn't been good enough. Was she good enough now, or was Whitney right? Had she only made the group because they didn't have enough girls? Maybe Sydney was sugarcoating things. What if her voice really wasn't good and she was about to make a fool out of herself at the mall?

"Here we go," Sydney said. *"You keep me spinning like a top, and I never want to stop."* Sydney tried to relax her by making goofy, crazy faces. *"But the world stops, stops, stops, when I see you!* Come on, Julianna!"

Julianna opened her mouth to sing, but then she caught sight of the lady again. Was she laughing at her? Why was that man buying a pretzel? Was it to watch her sing off-key? Why was that mother with the stroller staring at them?

Cocoa started barking wildly and it felt like a warning: *Don't do it! Don't make a fool of yourself!*

The mall started to spin. Julianna closed her eyes and tried to breathe.

Then she did the one thing she'd gotten way too good at. She quit before she even sang a single note.

CHAPTER SEVENTEEN

Sydney

When Sydney walked out of class that afternoon, Griffin was waiting for her.

"Hi! Why are you—I mean—" Sydney immediately scanned the halls for Lidia. She could still picture Lidia's face when she came across Sydney and Griffin sitting so close at the piano two weeks ago. Sydney had been avoiding Griffin's texts to get together or have dinner ever since. It had been twelve long days.

"We're supposed to rehearse for the music festival, remember?" he said.

She smacked herself in the head and her plaid headband fell off. She'd forgotten about her rehearsal with Griffin! "Let me grab my music notes from my locker and I'll meet you in the theater center." He stepped in front of her.

"No need," he said. "We're not practicing on campus today." She looked at him quizzically and he grinned. "We're taking a surprise musical field trip."

Sydney couldn't help thinking how great his smile was, but she didn't want him to know that. Instead, she tried to look mad. "You're not trying to take me on a date, are you?"

Griffin pretended to look horrified. "A date with you? Why would I want to take you on one of those?" They both couldn't help but blush.

"So where are we going, then?" Sydney asked.

"You'll see." Griffin's hazel eyes pierced through her. "It's just a short bus ride away."

Twenty minutes later, Sydney was standing in front of a restaurant.

"This certainly looks like a date," she said.

"We need food while we practice, don't we?"

"We haven't eaten during practice before."

"We've only had one practice."

She was running out of excuses. "What's Cliff Notes?" she asked, looking at the restaurant's sign. The place was near the last bus stop in Naples. From the outside, it looked like a dusty, moldy club that senior citizens in Naples frequented to catch an early-bird special. This was his idea of a first date?

This is not a date, she reminded herself.

I wish it were one.

"I'm not hungry," Sydney said. She actually was.

"They've got the best burgers in town." Griffin opened the door and she peered inside. The room looked dark and musty, just as she suspected. "Your oasis awaits."

Sydney's eyes slowly adjusted to the light. It felt like she had stepped back in time. The decor was dated with lots of wood paneling, vinyl booths, and low lighting. Several of the booths were actually full of older patrons. As soon as they saw them walk in, people shouted, "Griffin!"

Huh?

Sydney watched in awe as Griffin walked over to a table with senior citizens and began hugging people.

"Hey, Gladys! How's your back?" Griffin said to one woman. "How's the golf game, Phil?"

He's like the mayor. It was actually pretty cute to watch.

In the center of the room, two pianos faced each other. One man was playing eighties tunes that reminded her of dentist office music. At the other piano, an older man was playing the harmony. He waved to Griffin.

"Hey, Grandpa," Griffin said and led Sydney over to the piano.

"Grandpa?" Sydney wondered aloud.

The man stopped playing and stood up. "So this is the young lady you brought to sing for us today." He shook her hand. "I'm Cliff. It's nice to finally meet you."

Finally? "It's nice to meet you too," Sydney said. Griffin had his eyes.

"I want her on my team," Cliff told Griffin.

Griffin laughed. "Okay, fine! I'll be with Herb. At least for the first round." He winked at Sydney. "May the best singer and piano player win."

Sydney grabbed his arm. "Wait a minute. What are we doing?"

"There's no way we're going to find the right duet to sing at the festival practicing on campus. There are too many distractions." Thankfully, Griffin didn't say Lidia's name as one of them. "Here, we can test out some tunes. This place is a dueling piano bar on Tuesdays." He smiled. "Told you this wasn't a date."

"So this is a singing competition?" Sydney was warming to the idea.

"Yep. You versus me. The crowd picks the winner. What do you say? Up for some friendly competition?"

Sydney looked around the half-empty restaurant. The room was dark and the crowd was all over the age of sixty-five. This was the strangest date-that-wasn't-a-date that she had ever been on. What did she have to lose?

She held out her hand to shake on it. "You're on."

"I hope you know Sinatra," said Cliff, sliding over on his piano bench to make room for her. "Have you ever heard of 'You Make Me Feel So Young'?"

"Are you kidding?" Sydney looked at the sheet music. "It's my grandma's favorite Sinatra tune."

"Great taste," Cliff said. "Is your grandma single?" Cliff gave Sydney a look she'd seen Griffin make before.

Sydney laughed. "Sorry. She's happily married."

"Too bad," said Cliff and they both laughed. Cliff started to play again. "Here's how this works: We sing a stanza, they sing a stanza, and so on. Sometimes the audience picks a song and the first person to start playing and singing is the one who gets to sing it, but sometimes we compete for the same song. Got it?"

"I know that drill," said Sydney.

Cliff played the first few chords of the song before Sydney started to sing. She could barely see the top of Griffin's blond hair from where she was seated, but when it was his turn to sing, she could hear him.

His voice always gave her goose bumps, and this was before she knew how good Griffin was at mimicking Sinatra. She was so distracted by his voice, she almost forgot to jump in when it was her turn. Cliff nudged her just in time and Sydney took it away. She had to admit—that Frank Sinatra had some good tunes.

When they finished the song, they waited for the restaurant-goers to vote.

"And the winner," said Evelyn, the waitress, reading from a tiny slip of paper. "Is Sydney and Cliff!"

"No!" Griffin shouted. "Herb and I were robbed!"

Sydney laughed as she and Cliff stood up and took a bow. Herb and Griffin walked over to shake their hands.

"As my prize for winning, I demand you buy me a burger and fries," Sydney told Griffin as they walked away from the pianos and let Cliff and Herb continue to play. "They look very greasy and very delicious."

"They are," Griffin said. "But if I'm buying, that's kind of like a date, isn't it?"

Her heart thumped hard and Sydney thought for a moment. It kind of was. "No comment."

They sat at a corner booth under a picture of dogs playing poker. For a while, they just watched Griffin's grandfather play and ate their burgers in silence.

"He's really good," Sydney finally said.

"He taught me how to play when I was three. I've been singing here with him since I was in kindergarten." He smiled playfully. "Kids under ten make great tips at a place like this."

His smile faded slightly. "But when my mom and dad got divorced, this place also sort of became our afternoon babysitter. Now I'm old enough to go home alone, but my younger sister and brother, Rylie and Kyle, come here on the afternoons I have Kingfishers practice. Grandpa keeps an eye on things."

Griffin had talked to Sydney about being a child of divorce before. They had that in common too and traded stories about vacation planning. Did Mom get the first half of summer break or the second half? Would winter break be spent in Florida where it was warm or Philly where it would be cold? Griffin's parents both lived in Florida, but about three hours apart.

"My mom just moved to days at the hospital and she has twelve-hour nursing shifts, so sometimes I attempt to cook dinner, but the twins prefer the burgers at Cliff Notes to my home cooking." He gave her a look. "I burn water."

She could picture Griffin doing his homework while helping the twins and attempting to cook dinner at the same time. It sounded impossible. "I'm good with pasta dishes. I make a mean smashed lasagna."

"Smashed lasagna?" Griffin didn't look convinced. "That sounds as bad as burned pasta."

Sydney feigned being hurt. "My little cousins love it. You break the lasagna noodles and cook the whole dish in one skillet. It's a huge hit, I promise."

"Can I get the recipe?" Griffin pulled out his phone and started typing. "I've got a whole Pinterest board full of kid-friendly meals." Sydney tried not to laugh. "Yeah, I Pinterest," he said defensively, holding his phone close to his chest. "They have easy recipes on there!"

"I'll give you the recipe, but why don't you let me make it for you guys?" Sydney suggested. "How about Thursday? I can bring it over. We don't have practice that afternoon."

"You don't have to do that," Griffin said, sounding funny.

"I want to." Sydney took another bite of the burger. It was the best one she'd ever had. She might have to bring her dad back here. She could picture the two of them eating dinner with Griffin and his grandfather. No, no, no! Why was she thinking that? She couldn't date Griffin! "It would feel good to help. I'm not doing much good for the Nightingales these days."

Griffin threw a fry at her. "Are you feeling sorry for yourself? That doesn't sound like the Sydney I know."

"I'm not feeling sorry for myself!" Sydney threw the fry back at him. She kind of was. "I'm just pointing out the obvious. My a cappella career is going up in flames."

"No, it's not," he said. "Repeat after me: I'm Sydney Marino and I am the captain of the Nightingales." He threw another fry at her.

She threw several fries back. She rolled her eyes and mumbled the words. "I am Sydney Marino and I'm the captain of the Nightingales."

"Pathetic! Say it like you mean it!" Griffin's fists pounded the table.

Sydney took a deep breath and shouted, "I am Sydney Marino and I am the captain of the Nightingales!" Wow, that felt good.

Griffin stood up and cheered. "That's it! I believe you now!"

"I think I believe me too!" Sydney jumped up and hugged him.

Griffin held her tight and it felt good. Sydney wanted to stay intertwined, listening to the piano music, forever. If she moved her head slightly, she'd even be staring directly into Griffin's face. It didn't take a genius to know what would happen if she did that. But she still wanted to kiss him. Badly. *Just do it*, her whole body screamed. *Kiss him!*

He liked her and she liked him. Would it be so wrong if they kissed again?

Sydney thought about it and began to pull away, her face inches from Griffin's. His breath was warm on her face. *Do it!* she heard her head scream, but then she thought of Lidia. Even if Lidia had dropped her and the Nightingales, Sydney still couldn't hurt her that way.

She pulled away. "I have to go."

"I really like you," Griffin blurted out. "And I think you like me too." Sydney looked away, her heart beating fast. "I'm sorry if that makes things weird with Lidia. To be honest, I barely know her, but I know you and I want to get to know you better because I think we could be really great together. Don't you?"

She did. She really did. Griffin reached for her hand. It would have been so easy to take it, but she pulled away. "No. I'm sorry."

Sydney was glad the room was dark. This way Griffin couldn't see her crying on her way to the door.

CHAPTER EIGHTEEN

Lidia

"Explain it to me again: What is cosplay?"

Lidia's mom was driving her to the Naples Seaside Hotel so she could meet Jack at the cosplay event. Her mom was having a hard time with the idea of Lidia wearing a Halloween costume in late September.

Lidia adjusted her blond Sailor Moon wig in the car mirror. "Think of it like a huge Halloween party, except it's not Halloween."

This was Lidia's first cosplay experience and she wanted to nail it. She had a wig with a red headpiece and extra-long blond pigtails, and was wearing a white sailor-style leotard and a short skirt with blue pleats, and she had a big red bow tied around her collar. She'd even bought white gloves with red trim that completed the costume. She gave her hair one more glance in the rearview mirror. Gah! Where was the little gold crown headpiece that went on her forehead? Had it fallen off? She felt around the seat.

"Sounds fun," her mom said. "It will take your mind off the audition. When do you find out if you made the competition team?"

"Monday, I think," Lidia said. She hadn't heard anything since she'd auditioned last week. Miss Pattie Ann and the other teachers had put Lidia through a series of routines and floor exercises to see her skill level. Lidia thought she'd performed well, but there were a lot of steps she didn't know, and it was hard to keep up with the routine they had given her twenty minutes to learn. Miss Pattie Ann said they'd have a decision for her within a week, which means she should have heard by now. She was glad she was seeing Jack to keep her mind off everything.

The crown! She spotted it on the floor.

"Did I tell you the Nightingales have a new co-captain?" her mom asked.

"What?" Lidia sat up fast. "Why can't Sydney be the only captain?" She stuck the crown back on her forehead with double-sided tape.

"Between us, Mr. Wickey doesn't think she can handle the group on her own," her mom admitted. "They've had a hard time deciding on music and arrangements, and they're not ready to perform at the Bradley Academy Open House next week either. Mr. Wickey finally stepped in and appointed Whitney as Sydney's co-captain."

"Whitney?" Lidia's voice was shrill. "Sydney can't stand Whitney! That's going to make things worse. She'll protest every decision Syd makes. She already fights us on everything!" She knew she sounded hysterical, but this was serious. "The group will go up in flames or Whitney will try to make Syd miserable so she quits and then Micayla will be co-captain!" She groaned. "Can you imagine the Nightingales run by Micayla and Whitney? The only thing they'll sing is Katy Perry songs!"

Her mom pulled up to a light and looked at Lidia. "It's not your problem anymore, is it?"

"But . . . ," Lidia said. "Mom, this is wrong! You know it is. Fix this."

"Mr. Wickey already did," her mom said. "Don't worry about it, Lidia. I'm sure the Nightingales will be fine."

Lidia knew they wouldn't be. Not with Whitney in charge. She couldn't handle the thought of it. Her hand flew to her phone. She came *thisclose* to texting Sydney, but what was she going to say? Heard about Whitney? I'm sorry?

Lidia suddenly had a thought that made her stomach queasy. Did she quit the Nightingales because she wanted to join the dance team or because it was an easy way to avoid dealing with Sydney and Griffin? Which was really more important to her: dance or a cappella?

Lidia wasn't sure anymore.

She really wished she had a nonpareil right now.

"This is your stop," her mom said, pulling into the valet circle at the resort. Lidia watched out the window as Wonder Woman handed her keys to the valet in front of them. Then Hawkeye walked by wheeling a suitcase.

Lidia put her hand on the door to get out, praying she could walk in her tall red-vinyl boots. "Mom?" she questioned. "About the Nightingales . . ."

"Stop worrying and go have fun," her mom insisted. "Text me when you need a ride home."

Fun. Lidia could do that, couldn't she? She slipped out of the car and headed into the resort. The lobby made her wonder if she'd been transported to Oz. Everywhere she looked—the check-in desk, the lounge, the coffee stand, the lines to get into the conference rooms—there were people dressed in costume. Babies dressed as Yoda, grandfathers done up as Magneto, girls rocking pleather as Black Widow. It was like hanging out at the coolest costume party Lidia had ever seen. There was only one problem: How was she going to find Jack?

Lidia felt a tap on her shoulder.

"My lady," said a guy, who bowed and removed his top hat. "Look at you!" He took her in. "You are the spitting image of Sailor Moon herself."

Jack! "So are you! Your costume is incredible! You look like you stepped out of the cartoon!"

Jack had on a black tuxedo with a jacket that made him look like a circus ringmaster. He had topped it off with a black cape that had a red lining. The white masquerade mask over his eyes was deceiving, but his smile was undeniably Jack's.

"You're not wearing your glasses," Lidia noted.

"Contacts," Jack said and pulled something out from underneath his cloak. He held a red rose in his white-gloved hand.

"Thank you," she said shyly, wondering why she suddenly felt hot in her thin costume. "So what do we do first?" There were signs pointing people to fan-gathering spots, autograph sessions, and comic book Q&As.

"First we get some pictures." Jack held up his phone to take a selfie of them. They tried several because it was hard to get their high headpieces in the photos. Finally, Batman came over and offered to take the picture for them. "That one is a keeper," Jack said, marveling at Batman's handiwork. They crowded around the phone as Jack put the picture up on Instagram. "We can say the Dark Knight took our first picture."

"Our first" means there are more pictures to come, Lidia thought, her cheeks growing warmer. Even with everything going on with Sydney, Lidia had been excited about Jack's invite. It was just the escape she needed. So was seeing him every few days. Lidia found herself looking for him on the bus, on the street in downtown Naples, and lingering in Kyle's shop in the hopes she'd run into him. When she did, it felt like she'd won a lifetime supply of nonpareils. He was becoming the perfect pick-me-up.

She watched Jack talking but couldn't hear him. She was too busy staring at his lips and wondering, *Are we friends? More than friends? If I like you, does that mean I don't like Griffin anymore? And if that's true, does it really matter if he and Sydney like each other?*

The questions overwhelmed her.

"There's an autograph session starting in a few minutes, or we can get something to eat first," she heard Jack say as he removed his mask.

"Cosplay conventions always have the best-named food. Abomination Burgers, Hulk Shakes, Spider-Man Fries."

"I could go for a Hulk Shake," Lidia said.

Jack lead the way to a conference room with concession stands, and Lidia ordered a Green Hulk Shake while he chose an Abomination Burger.

"I'd let you taste mine, but I think I'm getting a cold," he admitted. "I've been working on this app for my coding class around the clock, and sleep seems to be the last thing I have time for."

"What kind of app?" she asked between sips of her green concoction. It was mint-flavored.

Jack leaned in close, a frantic energy seeming to take over him. "Imagine you needed to find a bathroom STAT and an app could tell you the nearest one. That's my idea." He bit his lip. "But it's kind of hard to set up an app for every bathroom in the country, so I'm starting small—Naples."

"I'd download that."

"What about you?" he asked. "Kyle said you've been in the shop every day lately. Are you taking a lot of classes like you wanted?"

He's talked to Kyle about me? "Yeah. I was practicing for an audition, so I needed to get in studio time whenever I could."

"How'd it go?" He sounded genuinely interested.

"I messed up on my last leap, but I'm hoping the rest of my routine made up for it."

"My Spidey sense tells me you got in," Jack said with a grin.

"Spidey sense, huh? What else does your Spidey sense tell you?"

"That you seem a lot happier," he admitted. "Did everything cool down between that guy you like and your best friend?"

The question rattled her, so instead she focused on the Charlie's Angels walking by with a pizza shaped like Darth Vader's helmet.

"Not really." Lidia felt weird talking about Griffin with Jack. "It actually got worse. The guy seems to really like my friend, and my friend and I had another fight about it so . . . I quit the a cappella group." She could see the surprise written all over Jack's face. "It's better this way. Now I have more time for dance."

"But don't you miss a cappella?"

"A little," she admitted. "I miss seeing the other girls in the group. Some of us are friends."

"That's a bummer you had to give up the group to get away from those two. Are they dating now?"

Lidia took another sip of her shake. "I don't know. I try to avoid being anywhere they could be."

"That has to be tricky when you all go to the same school," Jack said.

"It is." She shrugged. "There's just not enough time in the day to go to dance and a cappella practice. I had to choose."

"Did you pick the right one?" Jack asked.

Lidia stopped drinking and frowned. "I'm not sure."

"This is complicated." Jack shook his head. "Much more complicated than losing Mr. Krinkle to a technology malfunction."

Lidia laughed. "No, losing your computer and your friends are equally terrible."

Jack pulled his top hat down on his head and motioned to the line waiting to get into the event. "For now, what do you say we forget about coding and crazy a cappella groups and focus on cosplay? We could start by attending a Q&A discussion about the pros and cons of superheroes wearing capes."

Now that was a topic she had a clear opinion about. Lidia smiled. "I'm all in."

CHAPTER NINETEEN

Julianna

Julianna was waiting outside the theater doors when Sydney arrived. She shyly handed Sydney a piece of paper. "I was hoping you'd read this."

It was time to stop hiding behind her fear. If she didn't find a way to open up to Sydney, her Nightingale career would be over before it even started. She'd be forced to sing "Happy" in the general chorus. She had to stop coming up with excuses not to sing or share her music. First step: Share one of her songs.

Sydney read the lyrics, a small smile quickly spreading across her face. She looked at Julianna when she was finished. "Any chance you'll sing this for me?"

Julianna's first reaction was to panic, but this time she wouldn't let it take over. She slowed her breathing and focused on the sound of her own heart quieting down. Then she closed her eyes and sang the first two stanzas, repeating the chorus.

"I can smell it in the air. I can feel it on my skin. The rain is

coming and I can't stop it. No, I won't stop it. Let the rain fall down on me!"

Sydney hit her in the shoulder and Julianna stumbled backward. "See? You're really good. The lyrics are great too! Why have you been holding out on me?"

"You think they're decent?" Julianna asked, feeling lighter already.

"Yes! And so is your voice." Sydney scratched her chin. "Maybe your problem isn't performing in public. Maybe it's trusting the people you're singing with. The people at the mall and the ones gathered in front of the cafeteria were strangers. Maybe if you're standing in the middle of our group, who you know and trust, you won't be so worked up." Sydney grabbed her hand. "Let's go in and try it." She pulled Julianna into the theater before she could argue.

"Okay, but practice started a half hour ago." They walked in on a rehearsal already in progress.

Sydney stared suspiciously at the group of girls in mid-song onstage. "Practice is always at three thirty. Who started early?"

"I did." Whitney had her hands on her hips. "This group is an aca-tastrophe and *I* need to whip them into shape."

"Thank God you're here," Gabby whispered to Julianna as Sydney rushed to the stage. "Save us."

"*You* need to whip them into shape?" Sydney questioned. "We're co-captains now. *Unfortunately*," she added under her breath. "Neither of us should be calling practices without the other one."

"She couldn't find you to tell you," Micayla chimed in like she was Whitney's secretary. "And there was no time to waste," she said to the others. "The Kingfishers already staked claim to three of our song picks for the season, including the Ed Sheeran one, and we have the Bradley Academy Open House in *less* than one week. We are going to look like fools up there if we don't listen to Whitney!"

"And Sydney," countered Gabby. "At least she isn't trying to stage a coup and make this group into a solo act."

"Guys, why does it have to be a competition?" Viola asked wearily.

"I'LL SOLO!" said Mercedes.

"Ms. Heel would love a solo too!" added Donna.

"Why didn't anyone suggest *I* solo?" whined Micayla.

"Guys, no one is soloing," Sydney rubbed her temples as if she had a headache. "First, we have to pick some more songs." She held up a list. "I have some here."

"Why should you get to pick the songs?" Whitney grumbled, pulling a list from her pocket. "I have song ideas too!"

Everyone was talking over one another, then at one another, then Micayla jumped in to defend Whitney, and Gabby and Viola tried to back up Sydney. It got so loud, Julianna thought about covering her ears. Then she heard a loud whistle.

"Knock it off!" Viola said gruffly. No one wanted to mess with her. "We have to start listening to one another, not trying to tear each other down, or there won't even be a group anymore."

"Come on, guys," agreed Pearl. "I've waited so long to get into this group!"

"We have to listen to Pearl and Viola." Sydney looked at Whitney. "This may not have been the group we envisioned this year, but we *are* this year's Nightingales. It's up to us whether we come together as a group or fall flat on our faces." The girls all nodded in agreement.

"We can start by holding up our hands when we want to talk," Whitney suggested. "Sometimes I feel like I can't even hear myself think when we are in the same room together."

"And we need to listen to one another," Sydney agreed. "If we don't want to make complete fools of ourselves at the open house and competitions, we need to start getting along, even if it's hard."

Whitney sighed. "You're right, but how?"

Sydney thought for a moment. "Why don't we start by getting a feel for each other's voices?"

Whitney nodded. "Let's try singing a song together."

"I have props!" Sydney ran for the box of pink wigs still sitting backstage.

"Props?" Micayla said with disdain.

Whitney surprisingly shushed her. "Why not? It could be fun." Whitney grabbed a wig and plopped one on her head. She actually looked good with pink hair.

Gabby put on the light-up sunglasses. So did Viola. Mercedes accessorized her wig and glasses with a feather boa. Julianna put on a wig even though her hands were beginning to sweat.

"How about 'Turn Up the Music'? Everyone knows that one, right?" Sydney asked, sounding serious even though she was wearing glasses that were flashing a rainbow of colors.

"Everyone jump in when they're ready," Whitney seconded, adjusting her wig.

Julianna wasn't sure she'd ever be ready.

"Take whatever part you want," Sydney added. "Go high, low, beatbox. Whatever strikes you. On the count of three." She blew into her pitch pipe.

The song was starting. Julianna was supposed to sing, but could she?

The harmony sounded messy at first. No one was in the right key and some of the girls mumbled the first stanza. Then Pearl came in with some percussion noises and added a bass. Mercedes's voice, which was usually so loud, came down a notch when she heard the other voices. Donna still used Ms. Heel, but her eyes were on the other girls. The song was starting to come together. Feeling emotional, Gabby pulled some of the other girls into a football huddle and their voices magnified.

Julianna couldn't help but start to tap her feet to the beat. The song was calling to her. So were her teammates. No one looked mad or was trying to take over the whole song. They were a group and Julianna wanted to be part of it. Her heart was beating, but not as fast as before. *Like you did with Sydney. Just open your mouth and sing*, she told herself. She stopped thinking about her nerves and focused on the other girls around her. Then she opened her mouth and started singing.

"Turn up the music. Let the sound guide you. Turn up the music. Don't pay any mind to the other voices in your head. Just focus on me and let the music take you away, away, away!"

By the time the second chorus rolled around, Julianna was singing as loud as everyone else.

As Pearl beatboxed the last part of the song's arrangement, the girls held the final note. When they were done, they all looked at one another.

All at once, the group started to scream and jump up and down.

"You did it!" Sydney said, tackling Julianna.

"I did!" Julianna said, amazed at herself. She'd felt something during that song she'd never felt before: free. She hugged Sydney tightly.

"That was fun!" Whitney said, sounding surprised.

"I know, right?" Sydney agreed. "Let's do it again."

Everyone laughed.

"But the Kingfishers are going to show up here any minute trying to steal our rehearsal space," Gabby said. "They've been showing up earlier and earlier just to make us mad and ruin our rhythm."

"You know what?" She looked at Whitney. "I think we should let them have the auditorium. This theater has nothing but toxic memories for us the last few years. We should find somewhere new to rehearse."

"So true," agreed Whitney. "Let's get out of here."

"Any suggestions?" Micayla asked the captains.

Sydney looked at Whitney again. "I have an idea if you're up for it."

Whitney's eyes were bold. "I'm up for anything."

Ten minutes later, they were standing in the school's indoor aquatic center. The swim team was away on a swim meet and the offices were open but dark. After a quick chat with the lifeguard on duty, the Nightingales were allowed on the pool deck. The lighting was dim and almost bluish in tone. The water was perfectly still. It felt like they were the only people on campus.

"Don't tell me we're adding synchronized swimming to our routine," Micayla said. The girls all laughed.

"Nope! Listen to the acoustics in here. Hello!" Sydney's voice seemed to reverberate off the walls. "It's the perfect place to practice a song for the open house. I think we should go with . . ." She cleared her throat. "I mean, *Whitney*, do you have any suggestions?"

Whitney looked at the others. "Why don't we stick with what we know? What's wrong with singing 'Turn Up the Music'?"

Sydney thought for a moment. "Nothing, actually. The guys would never try to steal that one."

"Donna, why don't you kick us off," Whitney suggested. "Your voice is the perfect lead-in with Pearl's beatboxing."

"Me?" Donna asked nervously. "You mean Ms. Heel, right?"

Julianna watched as Sydney and Whitney looked at each other. They were actually communicating.

"We think you can do it without her, but it's up to you," Sydney said. "Your voice is even better than Ms. Heel's." She winked.

"Let's figure out an arrangement together," Whitney said. "One more time as a free-for-all, then we can start breaking it down. Sound good?" Sydney nodded.

Sydney pulled out her pitch pipe and blew into it. Julianna and the others followed the note and the sound of their voices filled the pool deck.

Then it was time to sing a second note. Gabby squeezed Julianna's hand and she got through the note too. Then she sang a third and a fourth and soon all the notes came together into a song.

Julianna breathed a sigh of relief. Looking around at the other girls, she had the funniest feeling the Nightingales were finally getting back in the a cappella groove.

CHAPTER TWENTY

Lidia

I made the dance competition team!

Lidia stared at the phone message she had just typed and contemplated whether to hit send.

As soon as Lidia got the call from Miss Pattie Ann that she had made the team, she'd started screaming and running around the house. Grandma Evie figured out what was happening and she started cheering and banging pots and pans. Then she suggested a karaoke medley to celebrate. They called Lidia's mom, who was still in her office, and she sang on the phone, as did Lidia's dad. Dougie grabbed his guitar and played along with Lidia and Grandma. When the song was over, Lidia realized that the person she wanted to share her news with the most was Sydney. Then she remembered they hadn't spoken in a month.

Do I send the text or not? Not, she decided, and she slowly and sadly deleted the words. She texted Jack instead.

JACK: This calls for THREE POUNDS of nonpareils to celebrate! Come early to Kyle's before class tomorrow and I'll buy. IF you share some with me, okay?

Lidia smiled. She'd see Jack tomorrow. This week kept getting better. Except for the not-being-able-to-tell-Sydney part. She typed the message to Sydney again. And deleted it again. Finally, she threw her phone on her bed in frustration, then plopped down on the mattress herself and stared at the water stain on her bedroom ceiling.

I miss Syd. Yes, she was upset that Sydney hadn't come clean about what happened with Griffin, but she missed talking to Sydney about ten thousand other things best friends always talked about, like the wedding disasters show they were obsessed with, or how annoying their parents could be about doing homework assignments days before they were due. She missed sending Sydney pictures of glittery sneakers she wanted to buy that Sydney would always talk her out of ("You're not twelve!") and the videos Sydney would take of herself singing audition songs months before she actually auditioned for something. She even missed working with Sydney on their pirate cruise tours. They hadn't had one together at Salty Sam's since the end of the summer. She could still hear Sydney trying to perfect a pirate "aye!"

But the thing that still caused Lidia the most "missing you" pangs was singing alone. She and Syd always sang together. They'd break out in song in line at Pinocchio's, at the supermarket, in the car, in line at the cafeteria, or in the airport security check line. She couldn't think of a place where they hadn't sung, actually. Singing with Grandma Evie and her family had its moments, but singing with Sydney was the best. When they sang together in the Nightingales, there was no feeling that could top it.

And she was giving all that up for dance.

Lidia sat straight up. Was she making the right choice?

This was the kind of decision she would have labored over with Sydney, agonizing over all the angles, and writing out plus and minus charts. This time she had made the decision alone. She thought of Jack's question again. *Which do you like more? Dance or a cappella?*

She threw herself back on the bed again. She wished she knew where Sydney was so she could talk about it with her.

Lidia looked at the clock. She actually knew where Sydney was. Nightingales practice was going on right now.

Lidia jumped up, pulled on some shoes, and ran out of the house, sprinting across campus. She didn't stop till she hit the theater doors and pulled them open. She didn't give herself time to worry about whether the Kingfishers were there too or what she would do if she saw Griffin. Somehow, she didn't even care. The only thing she did care about was seeing Sydney and figuring out a way to talk through all their drama. She bet Sydney was hurting too. Sydney would hate the idea of co-captaining with Whitney. They probably spent their whole practices fighting.

But as soon as Lidia pulled open the doors, she realized she'd been wrong.

The Nightingales were huddled together onstage wearing pink wigs and light-up sunglasses, and Sydney and Whitney were standing close together talking. Not yelling. Talking. Like they were getting along. She watched Sydney blow into her pitch pipe before the girls started singing a familiar song called "Turn Up the Music." They didn't sound pitchy or disjointed. They sounded really good. Lidia watched as the group got tighter and tighter, forming a small circle, as they sang in harmony. When they were done with the song, they actually cheered.

Lidia couldn't have been more wrong about things. Sydney and the Nightingales looked and sounded happy.

Lidia quietly backed out of the auditorium without being seen. It was clear the group had moved on without her.

CHAPTER TWENTY-ONE

Sydney

No matter how much Sydney appealed to the a cappella gods, Friday still came and with it the Bradley Academy Open House.

Like most private schools, Bradley pulled out all the stops when it came to opening its doors to prospective new students. All morning tour groups had been walking around the quad, which was decorated with welcome banners and navy and gold balloons. She'd been stopped several times by kids who had lost their group, and she had gotten stuck behind slow-moving parents carrying brochures and marveling at the school's new turf football field. Sydney had to duck and weave around them all morning to get to class on time. Not that she could keep her mind on schoolwork.

This would be *her* Nightingales' first performance as a group in public. While she and Whitney were playing nice, they disagreed on just about everything and the girls were still arguing over individual parts. What if Mercedes didn't remember to rein in her loud voice like Sydney and she had been practicing? What if Julianna got stage fright again? What if the whole school made fun of Donna, who wouldn't part with her Sharpie-designed Ms. Heel?

At least the song they'd been practicing sounded decent. After daily practices during lunch hour and after school, Whitney and Sydney had come up with an arrangement of the song that worked. It turned out Pearl was their hidden talent. Her beatboxing took the song to a whole new level. Now Sydney just prayed they could pull it off.

Sydney waited by the fountain outside the theater for the other girls to arrive. They were going to walk together over to the courtyard where Bradley had put up an outdoor stage. She pulled herself up on the fountain bench and swung her legs anxiously. She was a wreck, and when she felt like this only one person could calm her down.

She pulled out her phone to text Lidia and stopped herself. She still needed that reminder sometimes: *You and Lidia aren't talking.* The truth was, no matter how bad Lidia had messed things up by bailing on the Nightingales, Sydney still missed her other half terribly.

She heard talking and looked up.

"Move it out, people!" Whitney said. "We're on in twenty and I want to be ready to walk out onstage early."

"Hi, guys!" Sydney faked enthusiasm. "Ready to wow Bradley?" Julianna looked three different shades of green. *Uh-oh. Do I say something or will that make her more nervous?*

"Ms. Heel is so nervous, she could throw up," Donna said.

Sydney wasn't sure what the appropriate response was to that. "I'm sure she'll be fine!" She might need to borrow Ms. Heel's imaginary barf bag and throw up in it herself.

"I still can't remember—do we spin right or left after the first chorus?" Gabby asked.

"LEFT!" said Mercedes as Pearl said, "Right!"

Micayla sneezed. "Does anyone have a tissue? I feel like I'm getting a cold."

"Do we have an actual answer on the spinning?" Viola pressed. "Right or left?"

Gabby burst out laughing and the other girls looked at her. "Sorry. I'm just thinking about the Kingfishers and the surprise they'll find in their performance jackets this morning."

Sydney paled. "Oh, Gabs, you didn't do something, did you? Performance days are off-limits just like audition days."

"But they went after us on audition day," Gabby pointed out.

"Because we went after their pizzas." Micayla sounded nasally.

Sydney was afraid to even ask. "What did you do?"

Gabby gave her a sly smile. "I might have left a carton of red ants near where they hang those gold coats they wear for performances."

Everyone gasped.

"Gabs, you didn't!" Viola said. "Those ants burn. They'll know it was us."

Gabby shrugged. "They can't prove it."

"Let's just get over to the stage." Whitney herded everyone along.

Micayla sneezed again. "Does anyone have cold medicine? I feel nauseous and I'm not nervous. I never get nervous."

"You just need air," Donna told her.

"We're outside! I'm already getting air," Micayla snapped.

Sydney snuck a glance at Julianna, who walked quietly beside her. Her normally sun-kissed skin had a definite green hue. "How are you doing?"

Julianna exhaled. "I'm fine. I think. I've been focusing on my breathing like you suggested. And I'm standing next to Gabby onstage and she offered to hold my hand. That seems to calm me down. I think I'll be okay. At least I hope so." Julianna stopped short when she saw the crowd gathered around the stage. "Wow. There's a lot of people here."

"Forget the people," Sydney said, hoping she could get through to her. "Just focus on your team. We know you can do this." Julianna swallowed hard. "If I were putting together a new team today, I'd still pick you. I want you to know that."

Julianna managed a small smile. "Thanks."

The noise volume increased as they reached the courtyard. There were so many students and parents packed into the area, Sydney could barely see the stage. Sydney had the lineup from Mr. Wickey so she knew the dance troupe had gone on first, then the band and then the orchestra. The choral groups were always last. Sydney stood on her tippy toes and saw the general chorus taking the stage. She wondered if Lidia was performing with them. She'd heard she'd joined, but she didn't see her. A few seconds later, they started a decent cover of a song from *The Phantom of the Opera*. The Kingfishers would go on when the chorus was done.

"Come on," Whitney said, pushing her way through the crowd with the Nightingales in tow.

Sydney followed, scanning the crowd as they walked. She knew it was silly, but part of her thought Lidia might watch their performance.

"Syd!" She turned around. "Wait up!" Griffin was waving frantically from across the crowd.

Sydney blushed, thinking of how close she'd come to kissing him at Cliff Notes. She didn't want to be distracted before her performance. She waved and kept walking. "Ready, captain?" Sydney asked Whitney.

"Ready!" Whitney narrowed her eyes at the group. "Don't screw this up."

Sydney cleared her throat.

"I mean, do great out there and—*ACHOO!*" Whitney glared at Micayla. "Great! I'm getting your cold." She sneezed three more times in a row.

"Have fun and sing it loud," Sydney told the Nightingales. "Wait!" she panicked. "Where's—oh, there's Julianna." Julianna didn't look happy, but she was still there. Sydney smiled at her. "You guys have got this."

The Kingfishers filed onto the stage from the opposite staircase. Sydney was grateful she didn't have to see Griffin and the others close up. They'd probably try to get into the Nightingales' heads before they took the stage.

"Ladies and gentlemen, our next act needs no introduction," Headmistress Sato said. "The Kingfishers have taken home more trophies than any a cappella group in this school's history."

The Nightingales collectively rolled their eyes.

"They tell me they're ready to rack up more this year," Headmistress Sato added. "Let's hear it for the Bradley Academy Kingfishers!"

The crowd went wild. The guys walked to the edge of the stage to shake hands with students. Griffin was still trying to motion to Sydney. What was wrong with him? When onstage, "Fake it till you make it" was her motto.

"Let's hear it for the best a cappella group on campus!" Dave shouted into the mic.

"I can't stand them," Whitney said through gritted teeth. Then she sneezed again.

"Guys, I don't feel so great," Micayla said.

"Look! They're not wearing their gold jackets," Gabby said with glee. "Those are their good luck charms. Let's see how they perform without them!" She laughed. "Ooh, Dave is giving me such a look. What, Dave? Prove it!'" Gabby yelled at the stage.

"Please let Dave's pitch pipe break. Please let Dave's pitch pipe break," Donna repeated under her breath.

"Guys, does anyone else feel dizzy?" Whitney clutched her stomach. She probably had a case of nerves too. It happened sometimes.

Dave blew into his pitch pipe and the Kingfishers kicked things off with the official Bradley Academy pledge, which they had turned into a unique rap. The crowd went wild for that one. Then they dove into a short skit about a cappella (were they acting now too?) and high-fived prospective students. Finally, they started to sing.

It took Sydney a moment to register what she was hearing. She heard the song. She knew the song. But it took her a minute to realize why it sounded so familiar.

"Wait a minute," Gabby said, slowly realizing it too. "They're singing our song!"

Sydney watched in horror as the guys sang and danced their way around the stage to "Turn Up the Music." Her mouth gaped when Dave turned and winked at her.

"Our practices have been compromised!" Viola said, holding Gabby back from rushing the stage. "They stole our number!"

"How? We haven't practiced in the theater all week," Pearl cried.

Sydney glanced at the stage again. *Griffin.* There could be no other explanation. He must have come to practice to talk to her one afternoon and heard their song. But he wouldn't have told the Kingfishers, would he?

Her heart beat wildly as she watched the guys crisscross the small stage. She had no idea how quickly they had had to throw the number together, but they were still in sync. Even their solos were stellar and included rap breakouts!

"Of all the down-and-dirty a cappella tricks!" Gabby seethed. "They're trying to make us look like fools!"

"Which is ridiculous, because we could have done that on our own!" Pearl declared. The others nodded.

Whitney moaned. "Does anyone else feel like the ground is moving?"

Micayla weakly raised her hand. "I do."

Sydney was too stunned to speak. Could anything else possibly go wrong right now?

"Hi, guys!" said Lidia, showing up on the side of the stage with a big pink poster board that said GO NIGHTINGALES! in block letters. "I came to cheer you on. Are you ready?"

"Go away, Lidia," Sydney moaned.

"But I just wanted to—" Lidia started to say.

"Not now!" the other girls shouted and Lidia shrank back.

When the Kingfishers' rendition of "Turn Up the Music" ended, the crowd went wild. Sydney felt sick. The Nightingales couldn't get up on that stage and perform the same song as the guys. It was too humiliating.

"Ready, girls?" Headmistress Sato asked.

"What do we do? What do we do?" Donna repeated over and over.

"We have to sing a different song," Gabby said. "We can't sing the same one."

"I feel sick," Whitney said.

"Me too," Micayla moaned.

"I know, but it's the only song we know! It's the one we've been practicing!" Donna said, her Ms. Heel hand flailing around.

"Quick! What song do we all know?" Sydney asked.

"Do you guys know the new Katy Perry?" Viola ventured.

"Not Katy Perry!" they all moaned.

"Guys? I seriously feel like the ground is moving." Whitney was starting to look as green as Julianna.

"And now a group that needs no introduction, but will get one from me anyway," Headmistress Sato said. "My beloved Nightingales, which many of you know I was a part of, are back and better than ever." She consulted her cue card. "And they're here this afternoon to sing . . . oh, how funny! They're going to sing the same song the Kingfishers did. I can't wait to hear their arrangement. Let's give them a warm welcome."

Sydney's head was spinning. She adjusted her microphone on her headset as the others did the same. Whitney looked out of it, so she couldn't rely on her co-captain for help. She needed to think of a simple song. *Any song.* Something classic they all knew. Her mind went to show tunes, but not everyone was a theater geek like her. They needed a classic. They needed . . . Britney Spears.

"Baby One More Time," Sydney blurted out. The girls looked at her. "Do you guys know it?"

"Sort of," said Gabby as the others said, "I think so."

"That's my favorite song EVER!" Donna said. "Ms. Heel and I will take lead! This is awesome! We're already wearing school uniforms just like Brit in the video!"

Ms. Heel? There was no time to worry. "Okay, sing it!" Sydney said. "You okay with that, Whitney?" Whitney and Micayla moaned. "I think that means yes. Okay, everyone onstage!" She shooed them onto the stage. "Sing the best you can! Use the same choreography as before!" She was starting to sound hysterical.

"But that doesn't make any sense," Viola told her.

"It doesn't matter! Just go! Go! Go!" Sydney was shrill as she pulled Julianna onto the stage with her. "You know this one, right?" Julianna nodded. "Can you do the melody with me?"

"I think so." Julianna's voice was no more than a whisper.

Julianna, please don't fail me now.

Whitney took two steps onto the stage and fell backward into Viola. Sydney couldn't blame her for freaking out. There were a lot of people out there, including the Kingfishers, who were watching with beady eyes, and Lidia with her stupid pink sign.

Now she shows up? *Now?* When she can't even help us? Sydney blinked back hot tears. She stared past the crowd and focused on the palm trees. She took a deep breath. Then she got into position. *Be Britney! You are Britney! Channel Britney!* she willed the group.

Then she blew into her pitch pipe. As soon as everyone heard it, they started to sing while Pearl improvised with her beatboxing. She sounded great, as usual. It was the vocals that were the problem. Everyone started the song in different parts. Sydney couldn't hear herself over the racket. She tried to hear her own voice to attempt harmony, but Micayla cut in front of her, pushing her way to the front of the pack.

"Hit me baby, one more time!" Micayla shouted unevenly though it wasn't the chorus. "Whoo! Whoo! Go Nightingales!" She did a split in the middle of the stage. The audience cheered, but the move threw the rest of the group off balance. Julianna crashed into Viola, who hit Gabby. Mercedes was singing way too loud while Donna's puppet was making quite the impression on the audience. *"Oh baby, baby!"* Now Micayla was running, spinning, and leaping across the stage like she was in dance class. Then she stopped suddenly and clutched her stomach.

Two seconds later, she ran offstage and threw up into a trash can.

Whitney was so busy looking at Micayla, she crashed into the podium and sent it rocking almost off the stage. The audience gasped. Viola thankfully righted the podium in time.

"Keep singing!" Sydney whispered, but as she did, Whitney had a sneezing attack.

"OH BABY, BABY!" Mercedes shouted at the top of her lungs. "COME ON, NIGHTINGALES! WHO WANTS TO SPIN WITH ME?" She grabbed Donna. The two banged heads.

"Oww!" Donna cried, and stumbled off the stage.

"Don't leave me out here alone!" Gabby cried, knocking over a mic stand. The stand hit Viola in the head and she hit the floor. Gabby quickly pulled Viola offstage to check on her. The feedback on the speaker made the audience jump.

Sydney could see Headmistress Sato on the side of the stage. "Shocked" wasn't the word to describe the expression on her face. Mr. Wickey looked equally horrified. Lidia was in the audience. She and Sydney locked eyes and the word "failure" came to mind. Sydney wasn't sure she could feel any worse.

Then Sydney heard laughter. She scanned the audience. It was the Kingfishers, of course. They could barely control themselves, and Sydney could hardly blame them. She, Pearl, and Julianna were the last members standing. The way things were going, Sydney expected Julianna to bail any moment now too.

Her a cappella career, along with the Nightingales, had just gone up in flames in front of the entire school.

CHAPTER TWENTY-TWO

Julianna

Everything happened so fast. Whitney and Micayla getting sick, Donna and Mercedes hitting their heads, and someone saving the podium from falling off the stage. Pearl and Sydney were still standing, but the girls were so distracted the song was wildly out of tune.

"This is it," Julianna heard Gabby say as she dragged Viola offstage. "The Nightingales are finished."

No.

Julianna couldn't let this be the first and last time she took the stage without having a panic attack. She'd finally gotten up the guts to go out there! And her new friends needed her! It was time to prove herself.

Sorry, Britney. But your song isn't cutting it today.

Julianna took a deep breath and stared out at the audience. Taking tentative steps to the front of the stage, she stopped at the center and looked at Sydney. Sydney looked apprehensive. Julianna couldn't blame her, with her track record.

Julianna winked at her. "I've got this," she whispered.

Her heart was pounding, her legs were burning, and she felt nauseous, but she also felt more determined than she ever had before. She could do this. All she had to do was weave her song in with the Britney tune. Julianna opened her mouth and sang the words she'd written.

"I can smell it in the air. I can feel it on my skin. The rain is coming and I can't stop it. No, I won't stop it. Let the rain fall down on me!"

Sydney stopped singing for a second and looked at her. Julianna knew they didn't know the lyrics, but they thankfully kept going with the Britney track. Pearl picked up the melody and started to beatbox and Mercedes slowly made her way back out on stage. Julianna noticed Headmistress Sato's facial expression slowly start to change.

"Let the rain fall down on me. Wash away what wasn't meant to be. Help me start anew. Find something crazy to do. Let the rain fall down on me!"

The crowd started to quiet down. Donna staggered back onstage to join them, as did Gabby and Viola.

Julianna was singing her own song all by herself and she wasn't trying to bail.

Someone in the crowd started to clap to the beat and others joined in. The moment was definitely scary, but with every new note she sang, she felt more confident. When she finally reached the end of her song, she let the last note hang in the air till the applause started. It wasn't massive, but there was applause.

YES!

Instead of fighting, which was the norm, the girls all gathered around Julianna for a group hug. All except for Whitney and Micayla, who someone said had gone home quickly since it was clear they had the flu.

Even Sydney was jumping up and down. "You are the a cappella queen! You saved us! Where did that come from?"

"I don't know," Julianna said with a laugh as relief washed over her. "I just knew I had to do something, and that was the first song that came to mind."

Gabby hugged Julianna tight. "You're a rock star! At least now we don't look like total fools."

"Just partial fools," Pearl said.

"I have no idea what song that was, but it was beautiful," said Donna.

"Why have I never heard it before?" asked Viola, who was holding her head.

"I wrote it," said Julianna shyly. "I didn't know what else to sing. We were in a free fall and Britney just wasn't cutting it."

"That's an original song?" Donna asked. "We should be singing that for competition." People mumbled in agreement.

"You want to sing my song?" Julianna said in surprise.

"Donna's right," Sydney said. "That song was way better than anything we've come up with for Turn It Up, and we have to submit songs to them next week. Whitney's too sick to weigh in, but I bet she'd say the same." Everyone mumbled in agreement. "But first we have to go kill the Kingfishers." The girls moved into the crowd to find them.

Julianna's phone started to ring so she hung back, moving away to answer somewhere quieter. "Hello?"

"Hey, Ju-Ju!" said Naya in her always-excitable voice. "I saw your post about having your first a cappella performance today and I wanted to wish you luck."

Julianna put a hand on her heart. That was so sweet! She had never been as close to Naya as she had Amy, but they'd become good friends in the months prior to Julianna's move. When she thought about it, she talked to Naya more now than she ever did in Miami. Actually, she talked to Naya more than even Amy now. "Aww, thanks!" She lowered her voice. "We just finished. It went well, considering I've never sung onstage before."

"Yes, you have, haven't you?" Naya asked.

"No, not unless you count my audition for Tonal Teens, and we all know how that went," Julianna said.

"Well, I've heard you sing Adele in the car and your voice is killer." Naya was so loyal. She cleared her throat. "That's kind of why I was calling. I don't think I've really been the best friend to you, Ju-Ju."

Julianna was confused. "What do you mean?"

Naya exhaled slowly. "I swore I would never tell you this, but I feel bad because you've been writing all these aspirational posts. I got the feeling you didn't think you were good enough to get onstage, and that couldn't be more wrong."

Maybe Julianna had gone overboard with the wordy posts lately. She'd found all these sayings online about "fear leading you to greater heights" or "Sing as if no one is watching . . . or listening."

"I'm fine," Julianna promised. "I was just trying to blow off some steam."

"Still, there's something you need to know, but you can't say you heard it from me," Naya said quickly.

Julianna stopped short. "Naya, what are you talking about?"

Naya sighed again. "I heard Amy on the phone with you the other day about being in the Nightingales. She made it sound like you didn't deserve to make the group, but she was wrong! You belonged in the Tonal Teens too. That's what I'm trying to say."

Naya wasn't making any sense. "I auditioned and didn't make the cut. Remember?"

"That's because Amy didn't want you in the group," Naya admitted. "She told them to cut you."

"What are you talking about?" Julianna felt confused.

"When you sang that Carrie Underwood song at auditions, you were flawless. Everyone loved you! I think it made Amy jealous—she told the captain that you were difficult and would be tough to have on the team. That's why they chopped you. I think she was worried you were going to steal her spotlight."

Amy? Her best friend? "You've got to be wrong. Amy wanted me in the group. She told me so."

"She was lying," Naya said. "I wanted you to know the truth. I should have told you sooner. You're a really good singer, Ju-Ju.

Don't doubt yourself just because Amy made you think less of yourself."

Julianna felt like her stomach was going to drop out from under her. She could have been in the Tonal Teens? All this time she had what it took to be an a cappella singer, and Amy had made her feel like a talentless hack. What kind of best friend did that?

But in a weird way, the news also made her happy. She *did* belong on that stage, and she had come to that conclusion without even knowing the truth! Julianna felt like she was bursting at the seams. She had to tell Sydney.

"Thanks for telling me, Naya. You have no idea what this means to me to know the truth."

"Of course," Naya said. "I'm just sorry I didn't tell you sooner."

"But you told me, and that's what matters. I won't forget it." Julianna's breath was coming fast. "Listen, I have to go, but I'll call you tonight, okay?"

When she hung up, she headed back to the crowd and spotted the Kingfishers squaring off against the Nightingales. Sydney and Dave were arguing when she walked over.

"That went beyond pranking," Sydney was yelling. "You completely humiliated us."

Dave held his hands up. "All's fair in love and a cappella, sweetie. That's what you get for infesting our performance jackets with ants."

"That only happened today!" Sydney protested as Gabby looked on guiltily. "Who told you what song we were singing?"

Dave only grinned wider. "We have our sources." He turned to the guys. "Let's go, gang. I'm not sure we should be seen associating with a failing a cappella group."

"Failing a cappella group? You're going to be a group of dead fishes after we get our hands on you," Gabby declared as the girls followed the Kingfishers out of the crowd, both groups still trading insults. Julianna hung back to talk to Sydney, but Lidia beat her to it.

"Syd?" Lidia walked up to her tentatively. "I just wanted to check on you. Are you okay?"

"Do I look okay?" Sydney asked. "Griffin told the Kingfishers our song!" She covered her face with her hands. "I'm so embarrassed."

Julianna and Lidia looked at each other.

"You don't know Griffin was the one who did it, do you?" Julianna asked.

"It has to be him," Sydney said. "No one else could have done it."

"Do you really think Griffin would do that to you?" Lidia asked.

Sydney groaned. "Great! Now you're defending him? You know what? You two deserve each other. First you ruin the Nightingales, then he does."

"I . . . ," Lidia tried to say.

"It doesn't matter," Sydney said, looking at Julianna tearfully, then walking away. "The Nightingales' days are done."

"What? No!" Julianna ran after her. She grabbed Sydney's arm to get through to her the way Sydney had done with her once before. "So what if we had a screwup today. Tomorrow we start again. I got up there and sang today! *You* did that! We're finally coming together. You can't throw in the towel now."

"I'm sorry." Sydney sounded choked up. "I don't think I can do this anymore." She slipped farther into the crowd and Julianna watched her go. She knew the move well—she had mastered it—but this time was different. Julianna couldn't let Sydney give up just when she'd started to believe they could do it herself.

"I'm going to go try to talk to her," Lidia told Julianna.

Julianna watched Lidia head into the crowd to find Sydney and wondered, *Would Lidia do a better job of changing Sydney's mind, or was this really the end of the Nightingales?*

CHAPTER TWENTY-THREE

Lidia

Lidia just missed the bus as it pulled away with Sydney on it.

Great. This whole thing had gone too far.

The catalyst for their problem ran up beside her. He was out of breath. "Wow. You girls run fast for a cappella chicks."

Lidia glared at Griffin. "Just because we can sing doesn't mean we can't run. It wouldn't hurt you to do some cardio. Helps onstage." *What did I see in him?*

Whoa. Had her brain really just thought that?

"The bus is gone. How are we going to find Sydney?" Griffin asked.

Lidia sat on the nearest bench. "I'm waiting for the next bus. The bus makes one loop and it only has a few stops. Chances are it will be the same driver, so I'll ask him where she got off and then go there to talk to her."

"Smart." Griffin sat down next to her. "I'm going with you."

"No way. I'm going alone."

"Why?" Griffin argued. "I need to talk to her too."

Because I need to talk to her about you. "Because you're the reason she's upset," she said instead, her tone changing. "You guys humiliated the Nightingales today! Wait till you hear from the headmistress. My mother is not someone you want to make mad, believe me."

"That's why I have to come with you." Griffin looked at Lidia pleadingly. "I had nothing to do with the Kingfishers poaching the Nightingales' song, I swear. It was all Dave's idea! I told him he was going too far, but he was still mad about the Nightingales' ant infestation in our gold jackets and he made a game-time decision."

Ant infestation. Lidia smiled. *Only Sydney.* "You guys came up with that routine today?"

Griffin shrugged. "Yeah."

Wow, the Kingfishers really were good. Not that Lidia was going to give Griffin the satisfaction of telling him that.

"So can I come with you? If anyone knows where she went, it's you," Griffin said.

"I'm not sure if that's true anymore." How could six years of best friendship go up in flames so fast? Sydney had hurt her and she had hurt Syd. Was there any way to come back from what they'd done to each other?

"She's been so upset about you, getting a new co-captain, the team. I just want to make sure she's okay." He looked at Lidia hesitantly. "I'm sorry if this all started because of . . . you know."

Lidia's face flushed. "We don't have to talk about that."

"Maybe we should," Griffin said hurriedly. "I had no idea you liked me that way. If I did, I wouldn't have kissed Sydney that

209

morning." He sighed. "We'd been spending so much time together with the play and we got along so well, I thought she liked me." He ran a hand through his blond hair. "And then that morning at the coffee shop, I just thought, *This is it. It's now or never. Kiss her.* So I did and she completely freaked out."

Syd had been telling the truth, Lidia realized.

"After that, things were different between us." Griffin actually looked crushed. "I didn't realize why she was so upset, but then I found out about you and how I'd screwed things up between you guys. I am so sorry about that. I think Syd really misses you."

"I miss her too." *He really likes her. And she likes him, but they're not together because of me.* Lidia waited for that same familiar hurt feeling to wash over her. The one that made her want to dance her anger out and run for the chocolate. But now chocolate just made her think of Jack.

She smiled to herself. *Jack*. The one who made her laugh when they met up at Kyle's Candy Shoppe almost every day now. If she liked Jack, did it even matter anymore if Sydney liked Griffin, and if he liked her?

"It's really okay," Lidia said to Griffin. She hoped he knew what she meant. It felt weird to go into detail. "I'm fine with you two being together. I know Syd really likes you."

"And you're okay with that?" Griffin sounded tentative.

Was she really okay? Lidia looked at her longtime crush again. Sitting this close to him at the bus stop would have been a moment she would have killed for a few months ago. There was no denying how good-looking Griffin was, but today her cheeks didn't flush. She waited a second for the usual flurries to hit her stomach or her tongue to get tied up, but neither happened. She was over Griffin Mancini. Wait, had she really just thought that? YES! She let out a tiny cheer.

Griffin looked at her oddly. "Are you okay?"

Lidia started to laugh as another bus pulled up. "Yes! I am!" She threw her arms around Griffin and hugged him. "Thank you."

He hugged her back. "Um, for what?"

How could she even explain? "Come on," she suggested, getting out her bus pass. "Let's go find Sydney together."

Griffin hopped on the bus after her and they took a seat in the front row.

"Lidia?"

She turned around. Jack was seated a few rows back. "Jack!" she said happily. "Hey!"

He didn't look as happy as she felt right now. Then Lidia remembered who she was sitting with. "This is Griffin," she explained.

"What's up?" Griffin said to him.

"Hey." Jack's face was hard to read. He looked at Lidia. "Are you going to Kyle's? I just tried texting you."

"I can't. I have to do something with Griffin before my dance class." She'd explain everything to Jack later.

Griffin winked at her. "We're off to save the a cappella world."

She laughed. "We hope!" She looked at Jack again. "I'll call you later?"

"Sure," Jack said, putting his earbuds in his ears. He turned and looked out the window.

Lidia leaned over to the bus driver. "Excuse me. Did a girl with long, curly, blond hair in a plaid Bradley uniform get on this bus earlier?"

"Oh yeah," he said. "She did the whole loop. Got off near Fifth Avenue."

Fifth Avenue—that's where Lidia's dance studio was! Was she looking for her too? Lidia felt suddenly hopeful.

"Then she got back on at the next stop mumbling something about someone not being there. I dropped her back at one of the Bradley bus stops." He scratched his chin. "I just can't remember which one."

"Wait, so she's back at school and we're on a wild-goose chase?" Griffin moaned.

"No clue," said the driver, pulling up to the next stop.

Lidia looked at Griffin.

"She's not going to answer her phone if either of us call," Lidia told him.

"She'll probably ignore our texts too," Griffin added.

"We should split up and find her," Lidia suggested. "Whoever finds her first texts the other one. Deal?"

"Deal. Let me take your number," Griffin said and put Lidia's digits in his phone as the bus stopped again. Jack stood up and started to get off.

"You staying on?" Jack asked her.

"Yes," Lidia said and started to say more, but Griffin interrupted.

"Do you think she's at Salty Sam's?" he asked. When Lidia looked up, Jack was gone. She'd need to call him as soon as she took care of things with Sydney.

"Maybe. I'll try it. I'm not sure where she is." They'd always known what the other was thinking, like their own special brand of ESP. But since their fight, they'd been completely out of sync. "You check campus and her house. I'll try work." The bus pulled up to the next stop and Lidia jumped up to get off. "I'll talk to you later."

Griffin reached out and squeezed Lidia's hand. "Good luck."

Lidia tried Salty Sam's and the dance studio, but Sydney wasn't in either place. *Syd, where are you?* Lidia sat down on a bench and wiped her brow. The fall sun was still hot in Florida and it was making her loopy. She needed to cool off. She needed . . . ice cream!

She stood up. Chocolate was what Lidia craved when she was in the mood for something sweet, but Syd was different. She loved an ice cream sundae, probably because she'd been raised in the ice cream business. Maybe Sydney was at Pinocchio's. Lidia half ran, expecting Sydney to already be there. She tried hard not to think about what had happened the last time they'd been at Pinocchio's, the scene of Lidia's first meltdown. She rushed into the ice cream shop.

"Syd?" she shouted.

People looked at her, but there was no Sydney. Instead, there was some guy she didn't recognize behind the ice cream counter and no sign of a girl in a Bradley uniform. Lidia sat down at a table near the door. Her gut was telling her Syd would show up. She'd wait her out.

She didn't have to wait long.

Ten minutes later, Sydney rushed through the door. As soon as she saw Lidia, she stopped short, while Lidia stood up so fast her chair tipped over. The two stared at each other for a second, then fell into each other's arms, bursting into tears.

CHAPTER TWENTY-FOUR

Sydney

"I'm sorry!" Sydney cried.

"No, I'm sorry!" Lidia was teary too.

"I screwed up more," Sydney wailed.

"No, I did!" Lidia insisted, hugging Sydney harder as they both cried.

"Um, could you two let us pass?"

Sydney and Lidia pulled apart. There was a group of people trying to leave the shop with their ice cream cones.

"Sure, sorry." Sydney pulled Lidia into the back room where the Nightingales meet and greet had been. It felt like a lifetime ago. She pulled the barn door shut behind them.

They both started talking at once.

"I looked everywhere for you," Sydney said. "I have been such a terrible friend. First there was everything with Griffin, then I was such a jerk at the open house. I shouldn't have taken my anger about our lousy performance out on you. Here you came to cheer us on with this nice sign and I barked at you to leave. I went to your house, the dance studio . . ."

"You went to the studio? I have a class there later, but I was going to skip it if I couldn't find you. I checked Salty Sam's too."

Sydney's eyes widened. "I went there too! How did we miss each other?" They both started to laugh. "It doesn't matter. I'm just glad I found you. I want to apologize for everything."

"I want to apologize first," Lidia interrupted. Sydney shushed her.

"Me first," Sydney insisted. "I'm so sorry about everything with Griffin. You've liked him for such a long time and I had no right doing what I did. I'm so ashamed," she whispered.

Lidia put a hand on her arm. "He told me he was the one who kissed you."

Sydney wiped her eyes. "He did?"

Lidia nodded. "We talked and he explained what happened. I should have believed you."

"I should have told you as soon as it happened," Sydney said. She grabbed a napkin from one of the table dispensers and dabbed her eyes. "I felt so bad about the kiss. I was so surprised when he did it and told me how he felt that I didn't know what to do. I knew how crushed you'd be so I tried to hide it and it backfired. I'm so sorry." She started crying again. "You have every right to be hurt and mad and never want to talk to me again."

Lidia started crying again too. "This is what I've wanted you to say the whole time!"

Sydney stopped crying. "What?"

Lidia laughed. "I wanted you to apologize and really mean it. You just tried to pretend like it was no big deal and that it was all Griffin's fault. Even if it was, it still hurt, which is why I was so upset. You're my best friend. Even if it killed me to hear that Griffin liked you and not me, I wanted to hear it from you. He really likes you, by the way."

Sydney shook her head forcefully and started babbling. "It doesn't matter. I would never do that to you. Even if you never spoke to me again, I would never get together with him. Even if we get along really well and he's incredibly sweet and good-looking. NO! I just couldn't. I wouldn't. I can't."

"Syd!" Lidia tried to quiet her down. "Do you like him?" She looked Sydney directly in the eyes. "Be honest. I want you to tell me the truth. Do you like him?"

Sydney could have lied. She didn't want to hurt Lidia any more than she already had. But if she kept lying, they'd have no shot at repairing their friendship. "Yes," she whispered.

"Then you should be together," Lidia said simply and pulled out her phone. She messaged Griffin to let him know she'd found Sydney and Sydney started to protest. "I want you to be happy, and if Griffin makes you happy, then you guys should be together. I'm okay, I promise."

"But," Sydney started to say.

"No buts," Lidia told her. "Don't fight it because of me. I'm okay." Sydney looked skeptical. "I promise." She hesitated. "I like some-one else."

"Who?" Sydney demanded. "Since when?"

"I met him on the bus," Lidia explained, her cheeks brightening. "He takes a coding class next to the dance studio so we've met up at

Kyle's Candy Shoppe. We've hung out a few times. He gets me, and if Griffin gets you, go for it. Please."

Sydney exhaled. "I'll think about it. For now, I just want to focus on us. I miss talking to you."

"I miss talking to you!" Lidia said. "And I've got some apologizing to do too." Her voice was suddenly shaky. "I'm sorry I quit the group and left you to deal with the fallout. I didn't think about the fact that you'd have to take on a new co-captain like Whitney or how my outburst would ruin the Nightingales auditions. I was being selfish. I know how important this group is to you and you had such big plans for us this year. I screwed them up."

"You didn't do it on purpose," Sydney said diplomatically. "The group was already a mess before you and I took it over. Getting good talent to auditions was a long shot anyway." She nudged Lidia. "And you know what? You were right about Donna. Even with that puppet, she has a great voice. And Pearl is beatboxing now and she's really good."

"I heard." Lidia nodded. "I'm sorry I made the a cappella season harder for you before it even started. I just didn't know how to handle being captain with you after what happened. I couldn't stand seeing you, and it felt like every time I saw you, Griffin was following you around like a lovesick puppy. It seemed easier to quit than watch the two of you together."

"Do you miss it?" Sydney asked quietly. If she and Lidia were okay again, maybe Lidia would come back.

"Yes," Lidia said truthfully. "But I wasn't lying when I said I had made another commitment." She smiled shyly. "I made the senior competition team at the dance studio."

"Lid!" Sydney screamed, hugging her again. "That's fantastic!"

"Thanks, but it's a lot of work, and we practice four days a week and have competitions throughout the year." Lidia frowned. "It would compete too much with the Nightingales' schedule. It's not fair for everyone to put in the work and me to just show up once in a while."

"I guess you're right," Sydney said, but she hated the idea of Lidia not being part of the group anymore. "It doesn't matter now anyway." Her face clouded over. "The group is finished. We'd never be able to pull things together by Turn It Up. I'm sure everyone is going to quit after how we humiliated ourselves at the open house."

"Hey! You're Sydney Marino! You don't give up that easily!" Lidia said gruffly. "Remember that time our volcano for the science fair exploded the night before it was due? After all the stores were closed? Did you give up? Nope! You Googled how to make a volcano out of stuff in your kitchen cabinet and we had a new volcano by the time we left for school the next morning."

"And it smelled like cake batter, which was way better than the original version," Sydney recalled.

"Exactly!" Lidia said. "Turn It Up is weeks away! You have more than enough time to get this group in fighting form." Lidia boxed in place, pretending to hit Sydney in the arm. "All you need is a coffee with a caramel swirl running through it, and I promise your mind will be whirling with ideas."

Sydney had missed their banter. Their pretend fighting. The way they knew how each other took their coffee. She was happy to have her best friend back.

"I know you're busy, but will you help me?" Sydney asked shyly.

"Of course! I may not be in the group anymore, but I owe it to you to get this group back on track. What if you made a peace offering—like free ice cream?"

"No, I already did that, remember? This has to be bigger. What's going to get people to show up for a Nightingales meeting on a Saturday morning?"

Lidia and Sydney looked at each other. "A free cruise," they said at the same time.

"Jinx!" Sydney said with a laugh. They were back. "Salty Sam's is perfect. They can tan and eat. There will be no stress like at rehearsal."

"Sam would probably give us comp tickets if we pick up an extra shift," Lidia suggested. "Once we're out to sea, you do your Sydney spin on things and convince everyone to stay."

Sydney picked up her phone to call Sam and get the tickets. It wasn't a foolproof plan, but with Lidia's help, she just might be able to pull it off.

The Nightingales might still be able to take flight after all.

CHAPTER TWENTY-FIVE

Julianna

Nightingales! Join me for a FREE voyage on the high seas! Saturday morning, Salty Sam's, downtown Naples, docks, 8 a.m. We have lots to talk about—over bagels. I'll even let you take pictures of me in my pirate uniform so you can humiliate me online.

After Friday's open house performance, Julianna wasn't expecting to get a text from Sydney about a free boat trip. She was actually waiting for an email from Mr. Wickey saying the Nightingales were shut down for the season. Maybe this meant there was still hope. Now that Julianna knew the truth about Amy and what had happened with the Tonal Teens, she wanted to compete in a cappella season more than ever. Her dream now was to go up against the Tonal Teens in a competition and leave Amy in the dust. That couldn't happen if she wasn't in an a cappella group.

Julianna watched her phone blow up with the group's text replies. "I'm in," everyone said. Julianna added her name to the list. The next morning, her mom dropped her off at the docks.

"Don't forget to wear your life jacket!" her mom yelled out the car window as she left her near the pier. "It can get choppy on the water when it starts to rain."

Julianna looked up at the cloudless sky and recalled the weather app forecast: 10 percent or less chance of rain. Thunderstorms popped up in Florida almost daily, but usually during the heat of the day, which was late afternoon. It wasn't even eight a.m. yet. "Mom, there isn't a cloud in the sky."

Her mom scrunched up her nose and sniffed the air. "I don't care what the weatherman says. Smells like rain. Be careful out there."

Julianna shook her head. She had a greater chance of encountering a great white, but she didn't tell her mom that. At the pier, the rest of the Nightingales were waiting.

"Where is she already?" Whitney asked as she slathered sunscreen over her tan arms. "Micayla and I had food poisoning yesterday from that burrito we ate and we're still here."

"I think our illnesses were brought on by embarrassment," Micayla told the group.

"Or by eating that funky-looking chicken in the cafeteria," Viola told them. "Told you that chicken marsala looked nasty on Thursday."

"Whatever it was, I'm here *early* like a captain should be," Whitney said. "If she's going to call a meeting without her co-captain's approval, the least she could do is be waiting for us."

"With coffee," Donna added, a fresh Ms. Heel drawn on her hand. "This is kind of early for a Saturday."

"I'm here!" Sydney said, holding up two giant bags from Don't Be Crabby's. "I've got coffee, bagels, and a special guest." She motioned to the girl on her right.

"Lidia!" Gabby cried, hugging her. "Does this mean you're back?"

"Not exactly," Lidia said. "But I want to help the Nightingales, so I'm all in."

Whitney folded her arms. "I hope you don't think I'm giving up my captain position."

"No one is going anywhere," Sydney said with an uneasy smile. "I'll explain everything when we get on board." She motioned to the gangplank, which a group of tourists was already walking up. Apparently, the cruise wasn't just for the Nightingales. It was open to the public, so hopefully that meant they'd all be on their best behavior. "Are you guys ready?"

Mercedes pushed past the others. "YES, I'M SO EXCITED FOR THIS!" she said so loudly that a seagull nesting on a dock post took flight. "DO I GET TO DRESS UP? WHERE IS MY PIRATE COSTUME?"

"I am *not* wearing a costume," Whitney said as she followed the group up the ramp.

"Me neither," said Micayla. "I don't even know why we're doing this. Everyone knows the group is done for."

"Says who?" Sydney questioned. "Julianna was amazing yesterday at the open house. If it weren't for her, we wouldn't have even had a performance."

Julianna blushed. "Thanks, guys."

Sydney gave her arm a squeeze. "You came through just when we needed you the most. I think that means there is some life in this group yet."

"What song was that anyway?" Lidia asked.

"I wrote it," Julianna said proudly. "I've been working on it for a while and it was the first thing I thought of when our performance went sideways."

"I wouldn't exactly call what we did up there a performance," Micayla said huffily.

"Julianna sang and Pearl beatboxed," Gabby countered. "If it weren't for them, we would have looked like fools."

"We *did* look like fools," Whitney mumbled.

"Who's ready for a pirate cruise?" Lidia tightened a red bandana around her head. "There are prizes for finding buried treasure *and* singing in tune." She motioned to the guy with the goatee waiting at the top of the gangway. "This is Sam, our boss, and pirate captain."

"The sea is looking mighty fine this morning, so let's get on our voyage and find some treasure!" Sam said as Lidia and Sydney passed out eye patches and swords.

Julianna squinted into the bright sun—*there's still no clouds, Mom!*—then began poking around the pirate ship. The fifty-foot sailboat, which was larger than a school bus, had a giant black pirate flag that said SALTY SAM and pirate treasure chests on the deck alongside pirate treasure maps tourists got to use on a stop at a small island where the treasure was "buried." Sam explained it was the kids' favorite part of the tour. The boat was half-empty, with just a handful of tourists joining the a cappella group for the excursion (apparently, the noon cruise was more popular). When Lidia and Sydney finally came back out on deck, they were in pirate ensembles. The Nightingales had some fun with that, taking pictures of both girls to post online. After a quick pirate sea shanty and a pirate oath, the girls were off duty for the ride out to sea. Julianna joined Sydney in the front of the boat with the rest of the girls.

"I know this group has had a rough start to the year," Sydney said, "but I think there is still time to turn things around."

"Are you kidding?" Whitney said with a snort as she stood up in front of the others. "The Nightingales are the laughingstock of the whole school. We should quit while we're ahead and forget competing this year." She glanced at Micayla. "Then, maybe in the spring, we can talk to Mr. Wickey about voting for new captains who can actually pull this team back together."

Gabby brandished her plastic sword at Whitney's neck, which was covered in colorful plastic pirate beads. "Let Syd finish or I'll make you walk the plank."

Julianna whistled in agreement and the others cheered. Whitney sat back down.

"No, the truth is, Whitney's right," Sydney surprised Julianna by saying. "We do look like fools." She looked at Lidia. "Our fight got in the way of us hosting great auditions and missing out on unique talent. The Kingfishers stealing our first song didn't help. Neither did the pranks or our group's infighting and constant competition. We've wasted so much time already that it would be easier to quit than to keep going. But you know what? I want to keep going."

"So do I," Julianna chimed in, smiling at Sydney, who looked grateful.

"I know this might sound lame coming from the co-captain who left the group, but I think you guys can still pull it together," Lidia said. "I may not be in the group anymore, but I want to help in other ways. Maybe I could choreograph your numbers."

"I'd love that, if Whitney was open to it," Sydney said and Whitney looked surprised. "Your say is as important as mine is now."

"Let's be real. You hate that I'm your new co-captain." Whitney looked doubtful. "You're never going to listen to me." She swiped Sydney with her sword. "You don't even trust me."

"You're right." Sydney brandished her own sword. "I don't. I think the first chance you get, you're going to try to make Micayla your co-captain."

"I like that idea," Micayla said.

Whitney clinked swords with Sydney. Julianna winced. This could get ugly.

"She would be better than you!" Whitney snapped.

"Duel!" a tourist shouted and people stepped in closer to watch. A cloud moved into view, darkening Sydney's and Whitney's faces, and Julianna frowned. The weather was changing.

"I can't be worried all the time that you're trying to backstab me," Sydney said as they crossed the deck, striking swords.

"And I don't want you to think of me as your Plan B captain," Whitney declared. "We're a team now, so we should act like it."

"You're right," Sydney said. She dropped her sword to the ground. Sydney looked at the others. "We have to start working together! We have our work cut out for us, but I think we can be ready for Turn It Up in time if we come together. We want to hear your opinions, but we have to make the decisions or we're never going to be a team."

"What if you're not making the right decisions?" Micayla asked. "You haven't been a leader so far. How do we know you're going to be there for this team?"

"Sydney was there for me." Julianna spoke up and the others looked at her. "I've got stage fright. You guys know that. I didn't think I'd ever get over it, but Sydney worked with me till I felt comfortable getting up on that stage." She looked at Sydney. "Not every captain would take a chance on someone who is afraid to sing, but Sydney did. She stuck by me when I needed her the most." She looked at the others. "Our group is a sisterhood and sisters stick together. The Nightingales should too."

"I'm with Julianna," agreed Gabby. "We need to come together."

The others chimed in, even Micayla and Whitney.

"Okay," Whitney finally said and shook Sydney's hand. "Let's make this official and take the Nightingales code of honor pledge."

"What's that?" Donna asked.

"It's kind of old-school, but you sing a promise to each other that you'll be there for each other onstage and off," Sydney explained. "I've got the words on my phone." Everyone gathered around to read them.

Sydney pulled out her pitch pipe. "I promise," they sang, "to sing as if my song will take flight, to dance as if no one is watching, and to honor my team like I do my family. Being a Nightingale is a privilege and I promise that I will help this team and my teammates soar!"

The girls moved in for a group hug and the tourists on board all applauded.

Julianna grinned. Things were finally working out. Then she felt a raindrop. She looked up. The sky had turned gray and the wind was picking up.

"Pirates!" Sam interrupted. "Please batten down the hatches! Ladies and gentlemen, I'm afraid we need to turn off course till this sudden storm passes." The chop started banging the boat around pretty good as the rain began to fall harder. There was nowhere to go but on deck. "We'll head back out after it passes, or you're welcome to take half off a future voyage."

Julianna's mom had been right. Where was that life jacket?

"Half off a future voyage? I just want to survive this one," Micayla said as she clung to Whitney.

Gabby grabbed Viola and held on for dear life. "It's the curse! It's going to send the Nightingales to the bottom of the ocean!"

Viola lightly slapped her cheek. "Pull yourself together! We're not sinking! We're not cursed!"

The ship leaned sharply to the left before righting itself. The wind picked up quickly, and a few of the kids on the boat started to cry.

"Okay, maybe we are cursed," Viola agreed, hugging Gabby back.

"We're not cursed," Sydney insisted. "Everyone stay calm."

"I need you guys to keep everyone distracted as we make our way back to the dock," Sam said to Sydney and the group. "Keep them happy. It's going to be a bumpy ride."

Julianna heard thunder in the distance.

"Keep them happy? How?" Gabby asked.

A bump in the water caused everyone to fall into one another. The little kids on board wailed louder.

"We do it by acting like a team," Julianna said, and Sydney and Whitney nodded. "We'll work together and keep the tourists calm."

"What's the plan, captains?" Gabby asked.

The rain began to hit them in the face.

Sydney conferred with Whitney. "We sing, of course. You guys up for it?"

The Nightingales nodded in agreement.

"Song?" Julianna asked.

Sydney and Whitney looked at each other. Sydney whispered in Whitney's ear. Whitney nodded.

"'Sit Down, You're Rockin' the Boat,'" Sydney told them. "Everyone know it? From *Guys and Dolls*?" The Nightingales nodded. "Great! It's one of my favorite musicals!"

"They're all your favorite," Lidia said and everyone laughed. "Mind if I make a guest singing appearance?"

"Glad to have you," Whitney said as they hit another big bump and tourists shrieked. "Time to sing. Jump in when you can."

"Mercedes, keep your volume in check. Pearl, beatbox us a great rhythm, and Donna, you and Ms. Heel knock out the chorus with the others," Sydney instructed. "Julianna, if you're feeling a solo, you and Micayla should go for it. Everyone ready?" She blew into her pitch pipe and looked at the group.

"I dreamed last night I was on the boat to heaven . . . ," they sang.

They got some of the lyrics wrong at first. Some of the girls didn't know the song as well as Sydney and Lidia did, but they all remembered the chorus. Viola knew a stanza no one could remember, and one of the tourists knew the whole song backward and forward. As the wind whipped the sailboat around, the whole boat kept singing, and the Nightingales were singing for all they were worth.

"Sit down, sit down, sit down, sit down, sit down you're rocking the boat!"

Standing and sitting along with the commands of the song, Julianna and the Nightingales listened to Sydney and Whitney for cues as if this was what they always did.

Everyone smiled as they finally pulled into the dock and the never-ending song came to an end. The tourists even cheered. Julianna and the girls all high-fived.

Julianna knew they weren't out of the woods yet. A big song-and-dance number in a storm didn't make all of the Nightingales' problems disappear, but somehow, Julianna had a feeling that they were on their way to getting their groove back.

CHAPTER TWENTY-SIX

Sydney

For once, the week flew by. Sydney couldn't wait to get to practice. It still felt weird not to have Lidia in the group, but she had to let Lidia follow her own dream. Even if it no longer was the same dream as her own. Now she had someone new to run ideas by.

"You ready to wow them?" Whitney asked when Sydney found her after school. Whitney had already changed out of her uniform and into jeans and a tee. She was standing outside the aquatic center with one hand on her hip, the other holding a stack of papers. They were song arrangements the two of them had put together the night before without causing physical harm to each other. Mr. Wickey had already approved them and none of the picks conflicted with the Kingfishers'.

The co-captains were making progress. Sydney still thought Whitney was rough around the edges, and Whitney said Sydney was high-strung, but they had similar ideas when it came to song arrangements. Especially one that had to do with Julianna.

"I'm ready to make a cappella history!" Sydney declared, and Whitney rolled her eyes.

"You're such a cheeseball," Whitney said and they both laughed.

When they entered the aquatic center, they were surprised to see the rest of the team already assembled. Viola and Gabby were walking around the stage singing to each other, and Pearl was practicing her beatboxing with Donna's help on vocals courtesy of Ms. Heel. Donna still wasn't ready to part with her, but Sydney knew they'd work on it like they had Julianna's stage fright. Donna had on a T-shirt with the Nightingales' new logo that she had designed after the boat trip. The logo was a birdcage that spelled "Nightingales" in the cage bars. The cage door was open so the Nightingales could take flight. Donna was ordering shirts for the whole team.

Sydney had a feeling they really were becoming one. Everyone seemed to be at practice to sing, not fight or complain about someone's falsetto or a silly curse. Sydney quickly sat down at the piano to help with pitch while Whitney instructed the girls on their parts for a Fitz and the Tantrums song they'd picked called "HandClap." The choice had been Whitney's idea, and Sydney had to admit, when Whitney explained how many parts there were and how easy it would be to get the audience involved in the handclapping, Sydney got excited. They worked on everyone's individual parts, then put it together as a group. Even though it was early, Sydney had a feeling the song would be a winner. After some song work, the group sat down to go over what still needed to be done before Turn It Up.

"We're going to keep working on the Fitz and the Tantrums song today and try the Ariana Grande song tomorrow, but we wanted to let you guys know the third song we picked for the season," Whitney told the group.

"Julianna?" Sydney called. Julianna looked up from her spot on the floor. "We'd like a Ramirez original to be our third pick for the season." The rest of the girls cheered.

"Really?" Julianna couldn't hide the hopefulness in her voice.

"Yes!" Sydney said. "Whitney and I loved that song you performed at open house. Who knows? Maybe someone will hear it and want to scoop it up. I'm still waiting for Lin-Manuel Miranda to call me for his next Broadway show."

"You know Lin-Manuel Miranda?" Julianna marveled.

"No!" Sydney grinned. "But I follow him on Twitter." The girls laughed.

"And you're sure you want 'Rain Fall Down on Me'?" Julianna asked. "I submitted it to a songwriting contest last summer and it was rejected."

"The judges obviously have no taste because it's a killer song," Whitney said.

"Can we hear it again?" Sydney asked.

This time, Julianna didn't hesitate. She was definitely starting to get more comfortable around them. She closed her eyes and sang the words by heart.

"I can smell it in the air. I can feel it on my skin. The rain is coming and I can't stop it. No, I won't stop it. Let the rain fall down on me!"

When she finished, the girls couldn't stop applauding.

"Nice, Ramirez," Micayla said, clearly impressed. "I'd be up for singing that."

"Seriously?" Julianna sounded surprised.

Micayla nodded. "Yes! Didn't I just tell you that?"

"I'm sorry." Julianna blushed. "I guess I'm still getting used to someone paying me a compliment for my music. At my old school, I didn't even make our a cappella group. My best friend had them nix me." The girls all sounded outraged.

"You don't need toxic people like that in your life." Viola smiled. "You're a Nightingale now." Everyone nodded in agreement.

"Great! Now that that's settled, let's try 'HandClap' again, keeping up the energy," Sydney suggested. "Mercedes, your voice is perfect to kick off the song. For once, we want you to be really loud." They all laughed.

Mercedes opened the song onstage alone and was soon joined by Gabby, Viola, and Donna. Pearl appeared next, her beatboxing loud and clear, thanks to her microphone. Little by little, the rest of the Nightingales came in. The group commanded the stage, spreading out to every corner instead of shrinking into a tight circle like they usually did. Mercedes's voice worked for this song while Micayla and Julianna had solos that highlighted their talents. Sydney could tell the girls were finally getting comfortable with one another. The mood felt like it had on Salty Sam's boat. This was the teamwork they all needed.

When the song ended, they heard someone clapping enthusiastically from the bleachers across the pool.

"You guys!" Lidia shouted. "You sound amazing!"

"What are you doing here? Shouldn't you be at dance?" Sydney asked.

"One of my teachers is sick so they cancelled the first class." Lidia said. "I thought I'd help you work through some dance moves."

"Maybe we should do a warm-up dance party first?" Whitney suggested.

"I'm always up for a dance party," Lidia said.

She quickly pulled Beyoncé's *Lemonade* up on her phone and the girls danced around, singing to one another. Lidia and Sydney spun each other around, and Sydney realized how happy she felt. Seeing the group come together like this was better than winning at Turn It Up.

Oh, who was she kidding?

She still wanted to win!

CHAPTER TWENTY-SEVEN

Lidia

Why were boys so weird?

Jack seemed to like her. If he didn't, why was he always buying her chocolate? And texting her funny messages? And inviting her to dress up as a manga character and hang out with superheroes and comic book geeks on a Sunday afternoon?

Except all that had stopped after their weird exchange on the bus that day she ran into him with Griffin. Jack still texted her back, but the answers were short. He didn't show up at Kyle's before their classes the following week like he usually did. When she jokingly asked where he had been hiding, his reply hadn't been funny. It had been strange, she told Sydney.

"What do you think happened?" Sydney asked as they talked on the phone for the first time in months. There hadn't even been a reason for the phone call. Syd had just called Lidia to ask if Mr. Kramer had been coughing all through English like he had in her class. Both girls were sure he'd just given the entire school the plague.

"I think Jack thought Griffin and I were together, but we were really only together to go find you." Lidia curled up on her bed for what she hoped was a long call like they used to have. "And I would tell him that if I ever saw him in person. He hasn't met me at Kyle's for ages."

"Yeah," Sydney agreed, "this is one you need to explain in person. You need to hunt him down."

Lidia's stomach felt funny. She finally liked someone other than Griffin, and Griffin was going to ruin it for her. She covered her face with her pillow. How had she screwed things up so quickly?

"Go somewhere else you know he will be and ambush him," Sydney suggested.

That could work. The next day, Lidia put a plan in motion. She was waiting outside the coding studio with a massive bag of nonpareils in her hand. Jack was definitely in this class, even if she wasn't sure which head was his. From behind, all the boys with dark hair looked the same.

A woman on the street passed her and did a double take. Lidia just smiled. She'd gotten a lot of stares that afternoon. When Jack's class ended and people exited, everyone looked at her strangely. Finally, Jack appeared. He stopped short when he saw her.

"Did I miss an email?" he asked. "Was there a cosplay event in town today?"

Lidia liked how he dressed now that the air was slightly cooler. He had on jeans and a graphic tee that featured a comic book character. He made no apologies for his love of comics. She really liked that about him too.

She looked down at her Sailor Moon costume. "Nope. I felt the need to try out my costume again before our next cosplay event."

"You look great," he marveled. "You'd definitely win a costume contest if you entered at the next event."

"Especially if we went together as Tuxedo Mask and Sailor Moon," she said hopefully.

She noticed his eyebrows knit slightly, but she was prepared for that. She took a deep breath and remembered what Sydney had told her during their pep talk: Be honest. It was something she was working on. Being honest with Sydney and with her family that dance had become the most important activity in her life. But she also needed to be honest with herself: She liked Jack. Why couldn't she say that and see what happened?

"Look, about the other day when you saw me on the bus with Griffin," Lidia said, tugging on one of her Sailor Moon pigtails. "Nothing was going on between us. There was this a cappella catastrophe at school that Syd blamed Griffin for, and I felt bad for her so we both went after her together. That's the only reason I was with him."

Jack nodded. He didn't look like he was convinced, so she kept going.

"Griffin and I cleared the air too. He likes Sydney, Sydney likes him, and I'm completely over Griffin and have been for a while," she declared in case there was any lingering confusion. Jack was still just staring at her. "He doesn't know his Iron Man from his War Machine. Huge problem in my book. The truth is, I . . . like you."

There! She'd said it out loud. She waited for the sky to fall.

Jack slowly smiled. "Yeah?"

Her whole body tingled. She tried not to fidget. "Yeah."

Jack shuffled his laptop from one hand to the other. "That's good, because I really like you too."

Lidia's cheeks burned. "Yeah?"

"I think Wednesday is starting to be my new favorite day of the week."

"Mine too," she said shyly. "I brought you something." She handed him a bag of nonpareils and a tan notecard.

"'Turn It Up dance competition two weeks from Saturday at the Naples Convention Center,'" Jack read. He looked at Lidia. "I thought you gave up your a cappella group."

"I did, but since I don't have my first dance competition till afterward I thought we could cheer on my friends together. I choreographed their number to the song 'HandClap.'"

"Fitz and the Tantrums?" Jack asked. "Love them."

He knew his music. Another plus. Lidia was proud of her first choreographed number. The girls had individual parts and group ones that required a lot of eight counts and quick timing, but they'd gotten the hang of it. Sydney had videoed the number the other day and sent the clip to Lidia. It gave her goose bumps it looked so good.

"I guess your bad luck streak is over," Jack said, reminding her of the conversation they had had the day they met.

Lidia grinned. "Everything changed the day you gave me those nonpareils."

"They are pretty magical." The corners of his mouth turned upward into a small smile. "And so are you." Her heart did a backflip. "I'll come with you to the competition, then afterward maybe we can get something to eat to celebrate."

Lidia looked confused. "Celebrate what?"

"Your former team's win," Jack said, as if it should be obvious. "And their awesome choreographer."

Lidia felt the hair on her arms stand up. She was going to the a cappella competition to root for her friends with a cute boy who liked her.

Things were definitely looking up.

CHAPTER TWENTY-EIGHT

Sydney

In less than one week, the Nightingales were taking the stage at Turn It Up!

In less than ONE week!

Sydney knew the girls were ready. They'd practiced their song arrangements for Julianna's song and "HandClap" more times than she could count. They'd practiced their perfectly choreographed (thanks to Lidia) numbers on the quad, at lunch, and even during a pep rally that week that Headmistress Sato had organized just for a cappella groups. Bradley usually never did pep rallies for a cappella groups, but Headmistress Sato had said she was making an exception. Sydney was proud that Bradley was the home of two a cappella groups going to competition, but she was still nervous about running into Griffin.

"You can't avoid him forever," Lidia had said. "And you shouldn't want to."

Lidia was being so good about this. "I'm too busy to worry about a boy," Sydney had insisted.

She was concentrating on leading her team to victory at Turn It Up. They only had a couple more practices before the competition, and Sydney wanted everything to be perfect, including her voice. She started with vocal warm-ups outside the aquatic center while she waited for Whitney.

Deep breath in and hummmmmmmm.

Lip trills! Tongue trills! *Hey, you walking by the fountain. Don't look at me like I'm nuts. I'm getting ready to perform!*

Deep breaths! In, out, in, out . . .

Now sirens and kazoo buzzing!

Buzz! Buzz . . .

"Sydney? Are you okay?"

"What? Griffin!" How had he snuck up on her? Her voice changed. "I'm fine."

"Lidia said I could find you here."

He lifted his backpack higher on the one shoulder it hung on. She tried not to stare at his white short-sleeved polo, which showed off his biceps.

"How are you? Ready for next week's competition?" he asked.

Sydney was still processing the "Lidia said I could find you here" part. Why was Lidia still pushing the Griffin thing? As she'd said a hundred times, she didn't need a guy in her life to complicate things. She was over Griffin Mancini.

At least, she told herself that a thousand times a day.

There were dozens of guys at Bradley just as funny and charming as Griffin, who also loved musicals and making music with their mouths.

She hoped.

"We're ready," Sydney said stiffly. It felt funny standing this close to him again. His coconut scent was overwhelming. Why did he have to smell so good? "Are you guys?"

He shook his head. "Not yet. There's one thing left to do. Do you have a minute?"

"I'm not helping the Kingfishers," Sydney said hotly.

Griffin tried not to smirk. "This isn't a Kingfishers thing. It's about the Nightingales, actually. They need your help."

"What?" she shrieked. What were the Kingfishers up to now? She had to put an end to these pranks! "Why didn't you say so? Let's go!"

"Come with me." Griffin offered Sydney his hand.

Go for it, she could hear Lidia say, but still she hesitated.

"Time's a-wasting," he said. "Don't worry. I won't declare my love for you in the quad or anything, if that's what you're worried about. I just thought I'd lead the way." His cheeks colored.

So did Sydney's. "I didn't think . . . I know you won't. I can walk myself." She kept her hand at her side.

Griffin looked disappointed, but he didn't argue. He took the shortcut across campus to the football field. People were running around the track and the girls' field hockey team was in the middle of practice. Sydney expected to see the football team too, but instead, she saw the Nightingales standing with the Kingfishers.

Aca-excuse me?

"What's going on?" Sydney asked. "Is this some sort of prank? Because we don't have time for anything like that. We are less than one week away from Turn It Up."

Griffin motioned for her to follow. "No pranks. Come on."

"Hi, guys!" Lidia sounded totally normal. She was smiling as she looked from Griffin to Sydney. And she was standing with the Nightingales.

Sydney was so confused. "Can someone please tell me what's going on?"

"Why don't you let Griffin tell you." Lidia looked at him.

"The Kingfishers wanted to apologize," Griffin explained. "It was wrong to steal your number and make you guys look bad at the open house. Bradley has two a cappella groups and we should try to get along. Right, guys?" The rest of the team mumbled. "Right, Dave?" Griffin tried again.

"We're sorry," Dave said with a sigh and snapped his fingers.

"We're sorry," the rest of the guys sang in harmony.

"Doesn't everyone feel better now?" Lidia asked. "There are two teams at Bradley and they should *both* do well at Turn It Up! It makes Bradley look good."

"You sound like your mom," Sydney mumbled.

"Lidia's right," Griffin chimed in. "We've all said and done things we regret. It's time for the a cappella groups to bury the hatchet and call a truce. Maybe if we go around and say what we're sorry for, it will help. Who wants to go first?"

Micayla sighed. "Fine! I'll go. We're sorry about the time we pretended to be the yearbook staff to get your worst baby picture and then plastered the pics all over campus."

Gabby snorted. "That was a good one." Sydney gave her a look.

"Dave?" Griffin pressed.

Dave rolled his eyes. "We're sorry about the time we . . . sorry. There's so much to choose from."

"We know," Gabby growled.

"We're sorry we posted your open house meltdown on YouTube." He exhaled. "Wow, I feel better."

"That performance is on YouTube?" Whitney freaked out.

The two teams started arguing again.

Griffin blew into his pitch pipe.

"Guys, this is getting old!" Griffin shouted. "From here on out, the Kingfishers and the Nightingales are no longer enemies. We're equals."

Dave snickered. "I don't know about equals."

Sydney crossed her arms. "You haven't seen our finished performances yet. We will blow you guys out of the water."

"You think so?" Pasqual asked.

"I know so." Sydney said and they stared each other down.

Griffin stepped between them. "As part of the truce, how about each team acts as the other's critique partner this afternoon. Turn It Up is this weekend, and this is the perfect way for us to run the number past someone unbiased."

"Unbiased?" Micayla mumbled.

Everyone halfheartedly agreed. "We will even go first," Griffin vowed.

"We will?" Dave asked. Griffin gave him a look. "Okay. Kingfishers, assemble."

"Who are they, the Avengers?" Gabby asked.

The Kingfishers walked farther out onto the football field and moved into a triangle formation.

"Now picture us in dark denim jeans," Dave yelled to the Nightingales. "Our hair is slicked back and we're wearing tight gray tees and black suit-jacket vests buttoned up with high-top black lace-up sneakers. We would have worn gold jackets, but they are being fumigated after the Red Ant Incident."

"Thank you for the fashion statement," Whitney said. "Want to name your stylist too? Sing already!" The other Nightingales goaded them too. Griffin looked directly at Sydney. His stare only made her more nervous. She looked away.

The Kingfishers bowed their heads, laced their fingers, and, one by one, started to sing. They mixed their beats till the song was entirely recognizable. Before long, Gabby's head started to bob, and Viola started clapping. Sydney swayed along with the other girls as each one mumbled some variation of "They're really good." Then Dave and another Kingfisher started rapping a different Sheeran song in the background. That's when Griffin stepped forward for a solo.

Sydney's breath caught in her throat. Hearing Griffin sing did that to her. She'd known she was a goner that first day at *In the Heights* practice when he'd hit a high note. The feeling only intensified through the summer-long production, growing as they started practicing for the music festival together. She thought of them together at Cliff Notes and her face reddened. A tingling sensation moved from the tips of her ears through her whole body. Why did she try so hard to deny it? Lidia gave Sydney a gentle shove in Griffin's direction. Sydney couldn't deny it any longer. She liked Griffin Mancini.

The football field faded away. It felt like Griffin was singing just to her. Sydney couldn't hear the other Kingfishers anymore. She wasn't sure where the Nightingales were either. Griffin stepped forward and grabbed her hand, and this time, she took it. He was staring at her the way he had on the summer stage when they'd been playing the parts of two people totally into each other. When Griffin and the guys finished singing, Sydney realized she was still holding his hand.

"The audience participation part is not in our actual act," Dave said.

"Go for it, Syd!" Gabby yelled.

Sydney grinned. Before she could think of anything witty to say, Griffin leaned in and kissed her in front of everyone. But this time, she didn't pull away. Instead, she let her lips linger on his even as she heard the two groups teasing them.

"Great! Our groups are commingling, which means we definitely have to be nice to each other," she heard Dave say to Whitney.

"I guess it was inevitable," Whitney added with a sigh. "Hey, how many of the guys on your team are single anyway?"

"Sorry for the PDA," Griffin said when they finally parted. "I couldn't help myself. I've been wanting to do that again forever." He hesitated. "Was that okay?"

She had Lidia's blessing, the Nightingales had a shot at Turn It Up, and Griffin Mancini made her feel like she was the inspiration for a Shawn Mendes song. "More than okay," Sydney said.

"Okay, Nightingales," Dave declared. "You're up!"

Sydney reluctantly let go of Griffin's hand and returned to her team. She, Whitney, Julianna, and the other girls looked at one another as Lidia watched.

"Ready?" Sydney asked the girls.

"Ready!" they all cheered.

Sydney stared out at the football field with a feeling of determination burning in her chest. "Then here we go."

CHAPTER TWENTY-NINE

Julianna

Julianna couldn't tear herself away from the side of the stage. The performances at the Turn It Up competition were electric and so was the crowd. Packed auditorium, balcony full of cheering fans holding up neon handmade signs, emotionless judges, and lots of parents geeking out in official a cappella team T-shirts. What wasn't there to like?

This was her first a cappella competition and she wanted to soak it all in, even the wackiness of the emcee. Rick D. thought he was a budding Ryan Seacrest. He smiled enough for all of them, flashing grins at every a cappella contestant he saw backstage, including Julianna.

"Ready to get out there?" he asked as he fixed the cuffs on the white shirt he wore under his suit jacket.

"Yes," Julianna said and she meant it.

Stage fright was not getting the better of her today. She had a score to settle. She had managed to avoid the Tonal Teens and Amy all morning, but she knew they were there and she'd have to face them eventually. She'd talked to Naya about the Tonal Teens' slight and Naya agreed Julianna had every right to be angry with Amy. But strangely, Julianna didn't want to fight with Amy. She just wanted her out of her life. Maybe that's why she had texted Amy the night before:

> You and I both know what you did. Our friendship is done. Good luck at competition—your team will need it.

Amy hadn't replied. She didn't call either. Julianna didn't need her to. Performing her original song in front of the Tonal Teens and wowing the judges would be revenge enough.

"How's our competition?" Sydney asked, coming up beside her.

"Tough," Julianna admitted. Each group she watched take the stage was better than the one before. Some would get a perfect score for stage presence while others had such intricate choreography they looked more like a cheerleading squad than an a cappella group. The vocals were too good to measure. Julianna watched the judges typing on their laptops for a reaction. They gave none.

"That's okay, we're ready." Sydney sounded confident.

"The judges and the competition people are always watching," Sydney had told them all earlier. "From the moment you hit that stage, you have to be ready to perform."

"Don't be over the top or fake," Whitney had added. "Be yourself, but not yourself, if you're going to freak out."

"Confident, but not overly confident," Sydney had added. "Do you guys know what we mean?"

Julianna didn't. This was all new to her. Her palms were sweating, her stomach was churning, and she could hear her heartbeat over the roar of the crowd, which seemed to intensify by the minute. Somewhere out in the audience were her mom and her grandmother. Mr. Wickey and Headmistress Sato had come too, along with Lidia and her new boyfriend, Jack. The Kingfishers would be rooting for them as well. The Nightingales finally had a cheering section.

There was a loud roar from the crowd as the all-boy group Vocalosity came running offstage. They were the Kingfishers' toughest competition. The Kingfishers had been one of the first groups to take the stage and had been done for an hour already. Julianna wished the Nightingales were finished. Why hadn't they been scheduled before the crowd thickened? Before the Tonal Teens arrived? Was Amy going to be watching her? What would the Tonal Teens think of the Nightingales' performance or Julianna's song? It was hard not to work herself up into a frenzy.

"And now, straight from Miami, the FIVE-time-winning Tonal Teens!" Rick D. announced.

"Don't look!" Gabby said as she and Viola walked over to watch behind the curtain.

"No, I want to see." Julianna inched closer to the stage. The Tonal Teens came up through the aisles, high-fiving audience members and taking selfies on their way to the stage. Amy led the way in the same hot-pink, form-fitting dress that all the members had on, even if it didn't look as great on them as it did on Amy. As she ran up the steps to the stage, she stumbled a second as she caught sight of Julianna.

Hi, Amy! Julianna thought with glee.

"Is that your former best friend and backstabber?" Micayla asked, coming over to watch too. "She looks petrified of you!"

"Good!" Viola declared. "She should be scared of the whole team."

Amy quickly recovered and blew into her pitch pipe. The group started to sing. The melody was infectious, which irritated Julianna. She'd give anything to see the Nightingales beat the Tonal Teens.

Julianna felt an arm snake around her back. It was Viola's. Pearl, Sydney, Whitney, Micayla, and the rest of the Nightingales put a hand on her shoulder or arm as well.

"This is the day the Tonal Teens' domination crumbles," Whitney declared. She could be scary when she wanted to be. "Just let them *try* to outsing us."

" 'HandClap' is good, but our original Ramirez number is going to blow them away," said Micayla. She started to sing the lyrics and someone backstage shushed them.

Onstage, the Tonal Teens moved in and out of formation, mixing Kelly Clarkson songs Amy was obsessed with. She had all the solos.

"There is no way we're going to beat them our first competition out of the gate," Pearl said sadly.

"Hey! Glass half full, remember?" Sydney said. Some of the Kingfishers walked over.

"We're going to give it our best shot. We're only going to get better from here," Whitney added.

"Or we're going to be banished to bingo night at the retirement communities," Gabby said. Everyone hit her.

"Maybe Salty Sam's can add an a cappella cruise," Donna suggested and everyone hit her too.

"It won't come to either of those things," Sydney said. "I predict we're in the top five today."

"Top two!" Whitney said.

"I'm going to make a prediction," said Griffin. "If both Bradley groups make it to the Orange Grove Championship later this year . . ."

"*When* we make it to the Orange Grove Championship later this year," Sydney corrected and he put his arm around her.

"*When* we make it to the Orange Grove Championship, the Nightingales are going to bury the Tonal Teens," Griffin said.

"I'll take that bet!" Sydney said. "The Nightingales are back and stronger than ever." She put her hand out. Whitney slapped hers on top of Sydney's and the other girls did the same. They looked at Julianna.

"Nightingales!" someone called backstage. "You're on deck!"

"We're ready!" Whitney yelled back. "Almost." Whitney motioned to their circle of hands.

Six minutes and twenty-two seconds.

That's how long Julianna would be standing under the hot stage lights in front of a live audience. Amy and the Tonal Teens still might walk away with a bigger trophy that afternoon, but they weren't going to steal Julianna's future. She belonged on that stage and she knew that now. Her music—whether it was meant for Beyoncé or the Nightingales—was her own and she would sing it loud for anyone who wanted to hear it. No one was going to tell her to throw away her shot.

Julianna finally put her hand in the circle. "I'm ready too."

The girls looked at one another.

No matter what their score was that day, nothing was going to stop them from being Bradley Academy's all-girl a cappella group. And if they kept working as a team, no curse would come close to darkening their practice room. They were going to claw their way back to the top of the a cappella heap. Amy and the Tonal Teens had better be ready.

The girls kept their eyes on each other and their hands stacked together, paying no regard to the Tonal Teens leaving the stage. Julianna knew one thing for certain:

She was a Nightingale and Nightingales soared.

CHAPTER THIRTY

Lidia

The sound of feedback made Lidia sit right up in bed. This time she didn't question where it was coming from. Especially when she heard a keyboard and a guitar come roaring in.

"Party rock is in the house tonight!" she heard Grandma Evie and Mom sing. *"Everybody just have a good time!"*

Grandma Evie and Mom were busting out "Party Rock Anthem"!

Lidia threw back her covers and jumped out of bed. She didn't bother to throw on her robe or grab slippers. She was not missing *this* jam session.

By the time her bare feet hit the bottom step of the staircase, her family was in the middle of the second verse in the dining room. Dougie even had on light-up sunglasses. There was the briefest of pauses at the sight of Lidia in the doorway.

She knew what they were thinking.

Would the girl who gave up being a member of the Nightingales still want to sing with them?

Oh yeah!

"Toss me a mic," Lidia shouted.

Grandma Evie gave Lidia her favorite gold one. "I was just warming it up for you."

Her mom and grandmother put their arms around her, and Dougie and Lidia's dad started to play again. Together they sang, *"And we gonna make you lose your mind! We just wanna see ya . . . shake that!"*

Around the dining table, the Sato women sang, creating a conga line like you'd see at a sweet sixteen party or a wedding. Some people might think it would be crazy to do this at the crack of dawn on a Saturday, but they had a reason to be up early today.

"Everyday I'm shufflin'!" they sang as the song closed out.

"Who wants eggs for breakfast?" Grandma Evie asked, still using her mic. "Lidia needs eggs! Or a protein shake." She looked at her granddaughter. "I already packed you a bag with water bottles and three protein bars. Maybe you need more. How many kids are in your group?"

"That's more than enough," Lidia said with a laugh. "I'm too nervous to eat. I'm going to run up and change so I'm ready to go."

Her mom swatted her with something. Lidia turned around. It was the *Bradley Buzz* newspaper. "You might want something to read while you brush your teeth," her mom said with a smile.

Lidia looked at the front page of this week's edition, which had just come out the day before. Lidia had already read the article—twice!—but she hadn't tired of reading it yet. She reread the headline: THE BRADLEY ACADEMY NIGHTINGALES ARE BACK AND BETTER THAN EVER! And underneath, in smaller print, it said: KINGFISHERS TAKE HOME SECOND PLACE!

The Kingfishers taking second place wasn't even the main focus of the story!

Ha!

Lidia bounced up the stairs, rereading the article as she went. The reporter, senior Tasha Stevensen, had gone to Turn It Up to give a firsthand account of the competition. Lidia suspected she thought the Nightingales were going to crash and burn and she'd have a juicy story to write about. She couldn't have been more wrong.

While the Kingfishers came in second place in the all-male division at the competition, it was the once-struggling Nightingales who became Turn It Up's true Cinderella story. After failing to place in competitions for the last FIVE YEARS, they came in third in the girls' category! Under the leadership of co-captains Sydney Marino and Whitney Corcoran, the Nightingales' rendition of "HandClap" and their choice of an original song by member Julianna Ramirez were both a capella perfection. Their hand movements and vocal performances were completely in sync as was the choreography, which was done by Lidia Sato, the Nightingales' former co-captain.

While the top female honor went to Miami's Tonal Teens, Sydney Marino says Bradley students should expect big things from the Nightingales in the future.

"The Nightingales aren't going anywhere but up. See you all at the Orange Grove Championships!"

Lidia knew Sydney would settle for nothing less. The Nightingales would make it to Orange Grove this year and give both the Tonal Teens and their very own Kingfishers a run for their money. And Lidia would be there beside them, cheering them on.

Downstairs, she heard the doorbell ring.

"Lidia, it's for you!" Dougie shouted.

Lidia pulled her hair up into a high ponytail, gave her bare face one more glance in the mirror (she'd do her stage makeup when she got to the auditorium), and grabbed her rolling dance bag that held all her costumes. The side was bedazzled with her name. Sydney had done the decorating when she'd come over the other night to have dinner. This was Lidia's first official dance competition weekend and she alternately wanted to throw up in her bathroom sink and scream spontaneously and cheer. Her emotions were all over the place. Lidia lugged the bag down the steps and tried to stay calm. Her mother and grandmother were waiting.

"We'll be there in one hour," her mom reminded her.

"The doors don't open till ten," Lidia said with a laugh. "You guys know that."

"I want to be the first one in the door so I get the best seat," said Grandma Evie, flashing her T-shirt at her. It said DANCE GRANDMA. Lidia's mom's said DANCE MOM. Dougie and her dad had refused the cheesy attire, but everyone was really trying to get on board with Lidia's new passion.

"Okay, I'll see you then," Lidia said, giving them both a kiss on the cheek. Then she headed to the foyer where Dougie was standing in the doorway talking to someone.

"Hey. All ready to go?" Jack grinned when he saw her. Lidia's mom had offered to drive them, but since Lidia's competition was at the Naples Convention Center and they were leaving really early, she and Jack had decided to take the bus together. Jack had said it would bring her luck since it was where they'd first met. He held out a bouquet of daisies. "These are for you."

"Thanks," Lidia gushed, smelling the flowers, "but I haven't even performed yet."

"I already know you're going to score top marks in every number." Jack frowned slightly. "And I thought the flowers were a better gift than me wearing the T-shirt your grandma made me. It said DANCE BOYFRIEND," he whispered. "I just couldn't do it."

Lidia smiled. "I don't blame you." She looked at the clock on the wall. "You're early, though. Want to come in for some breakfast first? Grandma Evie made enough to feed an army."

"Good," Jack said, and swung the door open wider, "because you're going to need a lot of food."

To Lidia's surprise, the Nightingales were all on her front lawn. At the sight of her, they started to cheer. They were wearing blue TEAM LIDIA pins and Gabby and Pearl were holding a huge bouquet of balloons.

"What are you guys doing here?" Lidia asked.

Sydney bounded up the steps, wearing a DANCE BEST FRIEND tee that had Grandma Evie written all over it. She squeezed Lidia tight. "We're taking the bus with you and Jack so you feel the support of the whole team! Won't that be fun?"

"Really fun, especially if you all sing," joked Jack. "I hope there's enough seats."

Sydney's eyes widened. "Jack is right." She grabbed Lidia's hand and dragged her out the front door. Jack took Lidia's bag. "We'll get breakfast at Don't Be Crabby's on the way and take an earlier bus so we can all sit together. We can't be late to your first competition!"

Lidia let Sydney lead the way and smiled to herself. After all this time, she knew better than to argue with her best friend.

About the Author

Jen Calonita graduated from Boston College where she majored in communications. This degree helped her land a job at a teen magazine where she got to interview several of her favorite movie and music stars. These days, Jen writes books for teens, including the Secrets of My Hollywood Life series. When she isn't working, Jen loves going running, taking pictures, and hanging out with her husband and two boys at their home on Long Island in New York. She also enjoys going on walks with her feisty Chihuahua named Jack, where she does her best brainstorming for whatever project she's working on next. You can find her online at www.jencalonitaonline.com.

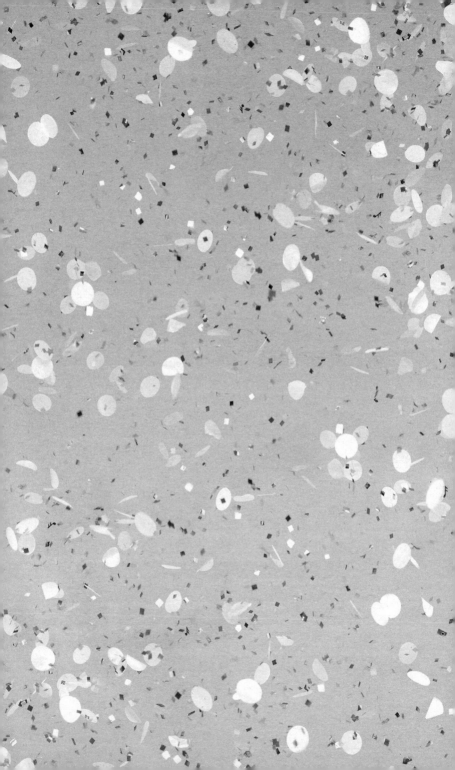